A ROGUE TO REFORM

ROGUES OF THE LOWLANDS
BOOK ONE

BY
HILDIE MCQUEEN

ARE YOU SIGNED UP FOR DRAGONBLADE'S BLOG?

You'll get the latest news and information on exclusive giveaways, exclusive excerpts, coming releases, sales, free books, cover reveals and more.

Check out our complete list of authors, too!

No spam, no junk. That's a promise!

Sign Up Here

www.dragonbladepublishing.com

Dearest Reader;

Thank you for your support of a small press. At Dragonblade Publishing, we strive to bring you the highest quality Historical Romance from some of the best authors in the business. Without your support, there is no 'us', so we sincerely hope you adore these stories and find some new favorite authors along the way.

Happy Reading!

CEO, Dragonblade Publishing

Additional Dragonblade books by Author Hildie McQueen

Can a Rogue truly change?

All Evan Macleod has left, after squandering his fortune, is a half empty country estate in the outskirts of Glasgow. He recruits a trio of friends and talks them into a plan to marry or seduce rich women to get capital and invest in a ship that is set to leave for the West Indies at the end of spring.

Felicity Murray returns home from two years in London. She senses something is strange about her brother's constant secret meetings with his longtime friends. She is especially annoyed to find he keeps a close friendship with the one man she distrusts, Evan Macleod. The incorrigible man has left a trail of broken hearts in his wake with little remorse.

In her bid to find a suitor and get his assistance, Felicity reluctantly agrees to help Evan in his pursuit of a widow, only to be horrified at realizing she's falling in love with him.

CHAPTER ONE

Glasgow, Scotland
March, 1823

T HE EVENINGS WERE the perfect time to entertain. Candlelight did its best to hide the peeling wallpaper, threadbare carpets, and fading curtains. In the daylight, however, it was glaringly obvious that the Macleod country estate was in dire need of reparations. Every place Evan Macleod's gaze landed made him wince at the stark reminders of his misspent fortune.

"Sir, your guests are inquiring about your whereabouts." Rosalie, one of two maids who remained in his service, hesitated at the doorway. "What should I tell them?"

He gave her a one-shouldered hug. "I am surprised they noticed my absence at all. By the sound of it, they are entertaining themselves quite well."

Indeed, a lively pianoforte tune and high-pitched laughter filled the air. His lips curved. "Tell them I will be down shortly."

Rosalie slid a glance to him, her brows furrowed. "Sir, the roof in the kitchen is leaking again. It must be repaired."

"What do you suggest I do?" he snapped. "I cannot afford the repairs."

Rosalie swallowed visibly. "I hope you do not find me impertinent, sir, but something has to be done. Your father would help. If you speak to him about it, sir. He will pay for the repairs."

"I will get the roof fixed," he replied in a gentler tone. "Get some rest, the front room can be seen to in the morning.

Goodnight, Rosalie."

There was a slight hesitation as the woman who'd served his family for many years seemed to consider saying something more. Instead, she bowed her head. "Good night, sir."

When the woman walked away, Evan let out a long breath. His father would undoubtedly cover the costs of all the repairs required to the estate. Not only because the house had been the Macleod family home for generations, but also as a lesson to Evan.

To teach him he had made a horrible mistake twelve years earlier when demanding his portion of the family fortune. In his arrogance, he'd told his father he no longer needed the family accountant to oversee his money and that he could manage it much better himself.

After graduating from university, Evan considered himself worldly and convinced he would multiply the money and live out his life in luxury without having to depend on his father's tutelage.

In less than three years, most of the money was gone. He'd been a rash and stupid nineteen-year-old who'd squandered the money on lavish parties, excessive purchases of items like carriages, clothes, and purebred horses.

At first, he'd been confused, stalking into investment offices and demanding to know where his revenues were. The bankers had tried to explain that it took time to grow dividends, and that by consistently withdrawing funds, he'd not gained money. He'd become enraged, insisting they'd stolen from him.

Someone probably had embezzled from his accounts upon noticing he didn't keep ledgers and would often appear inebriated when withdrawing money.

In truth, Evan had no memory of what he'd done most of those days.

Several times, his older brother, Richard, and their father had come to the estate with advice, attempting to help, and each time he'd laughed in their faces, bragging on his investments and how much richer he would be than them.

Evan turned away at the memories and looked up at the portrait of his grandfather, one of many family depictions that remained in the house.

"I have lost almost everything. But I will turn things around. Once I do, I will apologize to my father. I promise."

He knew it was stupid to not have apologized yet. Shame did strange things to a man.

His father, a kindhearted man, had not held any resentment. Evan was welcome to come home at any time. However, although invited to family celebrations, dinners, and such, he seldom attended.

On the rare occasion he did, Evan had done what he could to ensure he appeared to be with plenty of means. Still too stubborn to admit defeat.

He lifted a sheet of parchment from the table and read over the notes his father hand given him. The neat handwriting outlining exactly what was needed. Evan's lips curved. Finally, a way to replenish his bank account. A way to recover from the brink of destitution.

"Yes," he stated into the empty room. "Yes."

With purposeful steps, he stalked from the upstairs parlor to join his guests.

"Henry, remove the wanton woman from your lap. Everyone, I have an announcement," Evan called out in a loud voice, entering the large salon. A bright fire in the hearth crackled, the shadows of the flames dancing across the floor of the candlelit room.

The pianoforte music stopped abruptly, and every person in the room except for two turned to look at him.

Heavy breathing and grunts sounded.

The woman who sat on his friend Henry Campbell's lap cried out in apparent release and slumped forward as his friend grunted, his face contorting as he completed his own.

"Away you go," Henry said lightly, lifting the woman who

straddled him, and then plopped her none-so-gently on the sofa next to him.

"Ladies," the butler, Norman, appeared with cloaks and hats, and soon thereafter guided the pouting women from the room.

Evan pushed an errant lock from his brow and pulled out the pianoforte bench that had recently vacated by one of the women and sat facing the piano. His fingers traveled lazily over the keys as his half-closed eyes moved about the room, meeting each of his friends' gazes, holding one for a moment before traveling to the next.

First, he looked to Henry Campbell, the youngest of the four, who'd lost his inheritance on a wager.

Second, he met Miles Johnstone's gaze. Lord Rosenthal was the only one among them with a title. Heir to a West Indies duke, who'd been granted the title directly by King Edward. Miles's father had moved to Glasgow from England before Miles was born to indulge his Scottish wife. The combination of heritage gave Miles an exotic look that ensured he never lacked female companionship.

The last of the three men in the room was Grant Murray, whom he'd grown up with. Grant was a contradiction. He was penniless by choice, had broken all ties with his family for a reason he'd never revealed. Now he lived there at the estate with Evan, spending his days, or one could say nights, sleeping with wealthy women who ensured he never lacked for anything. Therefore, Grant had plenty of extravagant belongings, but no money to call his own.

The men, used to his abrupt announcements, were unfazed by his dismissal of the women, whom they'd paid to accompany them for the evening, and remained silent as he considered what to say.

It was already rather late, well past midnight.

"What have you been doing?" Henry asked, buttoning up his britches. "You did not partake of the...entertainment."

Evan rolled his eyes. "I have been working on something that is far more important. Which I am about to share with you, my three closest friends."

Although he and the others often gathered to enjoy the attentions of prostitutes, or other women who enjoyed the company of men without attachments, that night he'd been too restless to take part.

Besides, in Evan's opinion, hours of empty conversation that would ultimately lead to a rather unimpressive fuck did not, to him at least, constitute a good use of time.

"What is the grand announcement of the evening?" Miles asked, his dark eyes traveling from Evan's face to where his hands now lay flat over the keys of the pianoforte.

It was hard to keep from shouting out the words. Instead, he ensured a calm demeanor and stood. "Gentlemen, I have found a way for us to make a grand fortune. We will be rich beyond what we can imagine."

"He found the elusive genie in a bottle," Grant Murray, the quietest of the group, expounded. "I say we play cards for the three wishes."

Henry stood and stretched. "As you are aware, I would win the game, and therefore, the three wishes." He turned his hand, revealing a deck of cards.

"It is doubtful," Miles replied. "Else you would still have your inheritance."

Unfazed, Henry smiled. "I am a fast learner, and all the losses taught me well. I have not lost a game in months."

"That is because no respectable gambling den allows you in," Evan quipped. He held up both hands. "Listen, I ask for but a moment."

"Very well," Miles said. "What is it?"

"A ship." He paused purposefully for effect. "There is a ship bound for the West Indies that has lost its sponsor. The captain has agreed to give us three months to come up with the capital to sponsor it."

Miles straightened and leaned forward. "Why would he agree

to wait three months? Those ships make fortunes; sponsors are easy to find."

This was the best news he'd ever shared. "Because my father saved the captain's life when serving the Royal Navy and he feels obligated. Over drinks, he and my father spoke about it."

"Yer father served in the English Navy?" Henry asked, his face twisted in disgust. "Do you honestly believe an Englishman will repay a Scot for saving his life? I doubt any Englishman would be that honorable."

Henry, an avid historian, hated the fact that the Scottish Navy was absorbed into the British Royal Navy in 1707. They were all informed of every sordid detail because Henry never stopped talking about it and other injustices he claimed to have been done to the Scottish by England. There was little doubt that Henry hated England.

"That is neither here nor there," Evan interrupted. "What is important is that we must raise the money necessary to sponsor the ship."

This time, Evan smiled widely. "I know your next question is how will we do it?"

"We wait with bated breath," Miles said, all but yawning.

After filling a sifter with brandy, Evan walked to the center of the room and held it up. "Spring Season begins, my friends. Desperate mothers will be all but throwing their innocent and easy-to-manipulate, well-endowered daughters at us. New widows will flounce into ballrooms burdened with the heavy weight of too many diamonds upon their throats. These women, my dear friends are ripe for the picking."

His friends watched him with varying expressions of interest, so he continued. "And there are always the women, married to extremely rich men, who will pay handsomely for a virile body. We, gentlemen, will sell our bodies or marry to raise the capital."

He downed the brandy, savoring not only the rich flavor, but also by the way he'd just struck every one of his friends into a shocked silence.

>>>><<<<

THE NEXT MORNING, Rosalie and the cook placed platters of eggs, thickly sliced bacon, bread, and fresh jam on the table.

"Thank you," Henry said when one of the women poured him yet another cup of tea. "I can pour myself from now on."

"This ship," Miles began. "What is the name of it?"

For hours the night before, his friends had questioned him about the sponsorship of the ship. It was apparent they did not believe him; either that, or they thought he was about to be hoodwinked again.

"*The Abigail*, the captain's name is Thomas MacFarland."

Grant straightened, his green eyes narrowing. "I have heard of him. His shipments are always timely, and his boat well-stocked with spices, sugar... Why would he not have a sponsor?" he interrupted himself by asking.

"Must I repeat myself again?" Evan asked, growing annoyed. "He gave me his word to allow us to do raise the needed capital, and I believe him. He plans to remain in town for the Season. Told me he has a family here."

Miles nodded. "We must meet him to discuss particulars."

"I will arrange it," Evan said. "Now, gentlemen, to the plans. There is to be a ball at the Theatre Royal this Saturday. We must procure invitations."

Being a duke's son, Miles was the only one who could do this. They all looked to him.

He frowned. "I believe to already have an invitation. I will accept and contact the patron and ask for you three. I am sure she will agree without hesitation."

"Someone who will do your bidding in exchange for a bedding?" Henry asked, lifting a cup to his lips.

"A gentleman does not tell," Miles replied, pushing from the table when the butler appeared at the doorway. "I will hear of your plans another time. I have an appointment I cannot be late for."

When he left, the other two looked to Evan, waiting to hear what his plan was.

"With my reputation, it will be hard to convince a dowered lass's mother I am committed. I will seduce a lonely widow. I do believe Sorcha Robertson will be at the event, she rarely misses one. This time, she will meet me, her next lover."

Sorcha Robertson had been widowed and had been out of mourning for over a year. Since then, it was rumored that she took lovers, but only for a short spell before discarding them. Too afraid of men hunting after the fortune left to her by her late husband, she was distrusting.

Quite attractive and in her thirties, Sorcha often dressed in bright gowns that were on the brink of being garish. Her penchant for bright colors made her stand out at social functions, which was perhaps her way of gaining men's attention. Although she didn't easily trust, it was evident she craved attention. That was what Evan would exploit first.

Henry laughed. "You actually think to be able to seduce that woman? She is wily and won't be easy to convince. She has no need for money or jewels."

"There are other needs that money cannot provide," Evan replied while cutting through the meat on his plate.

His friends exchanged bland looks.

"What about you, Henry? Who would you target?" Evan asked.

His friend looked up to the ceiling. "With my family ties, I do believe to be an attractive match for some simpering young debutante. I will hunt for the perfect one at the ball."

"Aren't you afraid to be bored by someone like that?" Grant asked.

Henry shrugged. "I have to marry sooner or later, and I do not believe in love; therefore, I will marry someone of my family's choosing and grow to care for whoever it is."

They turned to Grant who yawned widely. Upon noticing

their attention, he shrugged. "I have no plan yet. I do not wish to marry, so I suppose I will be the one who will sell my body to some rich lonely wife or widow, or perhaps both."

"Instead of clothes or gifts, this time ensure to get coin," Evan said with a pointed look.

Grant let out a long-exaggerated sigh. "If I must."

IT WAS MIDAFTERNOON, and Evan remained in his study. There was little to do that day; however, with his mind awhirl with the current plan, he reviewed his ledgers in preparation of what he'd do once he had the money to take care of everything that needed attention.

"Sir, the men arrived and are repairing the roof over the kitchen," Norman, his butler, informed him two days later. "May I have them repair the hole over the servants' quarters? They tire of emptying buckets when it rains."

Evan glanced to his tattered ledger before responding. "Yes. Very well. Nothing more."

Norman nodded and turned away, stopping when Evan called his name.

"Why had you not told me of the leak in the servants' quarters?"

His butler, who'd served for his grandfather, gave him a soft shrug. "There are only three of us and we moved from the ones with the leak. However, the last storm caused leaks in our current spaces."

"You think me a fool for losing my money, don't you?"

The butler's gaze was warm. "It is the way of young men to learn from experience." Crinkles appeared at the corners of his eyes. "The women and I thank you for the additional amount in our pay this month."

Evan nodded. "It is less than each of you deserve. I know you work very hard."

The butler walked out, and Evan went to his ledger. There was enough to pay for the roof repair, wages, and food for the two months. Thankfully, one of his investments into a tobacco shipper from America continued to pay something regularly. If only he'd bought a larger share when he had the means, he would be living much better.

He grunted when Grant walked through the door without knocking. "Just delivered."

"What is it?" Evan asked, glancing at the envelopes in Grant's hands.

"Our invitations to the Spring Ball."

CHAPTER TWO

ONE BY ONE, pristine carriages lined Queen Street and slowly pulled up to the Theatre Royal. The first major event of the spring Season was in full swing, and every prominent household was to be represented.

Women in extravagant gowns, intricate hairdos, wearing sparkling jewels on throats, ears, and wrists were assisted from the carriages.

Upon entering, every guest paused in the ornate foyer until each family was announced by a man with a robust voice.

The din of excited conversations competed with the elegant string music that wafted from one room to the other.

Huge chandeliers shined brightly, as well as the candelabrums that had been placed here and there on large surfaces among the elaborate floral arrangements.

Servants moved through the throng, deftly avoiding feathers in hair and wide skirts as they served wine in crystal flutes and canapes from shiny trays.

Already several debutantes were standing out as the ones to watch. Beautiful young women with just the perfect look and sizable dowry. Their proud mothers kept a keen eye on the men who approached their daughters, each with hopes of an invitation for tea the following day.

Evan entered the large space through the arched front door, and not wishing to attract attention, skirted around the man who called out announcements.

Foremost on his mind was to find and study the widow Robertson. See what caught her notice and find a way to meet her in a fashion that would seem accidental.

It was only moments later that the woman's name was announced. Resplendent in a tangerine gown, with contrasting emeralds draped on her throat and dangling from her ears, the attractive widow entered the room.

Somehow, the colors suited the brunette, who stood silently while her name was called. Her sharp gaze scanned the room as a light smile played on her lips.

She was immediately greeted by a pair of women who seemed to know her well and were probably recruited to avoid her remaining alone while walking about the room.

Evan moved around an annoyingly large vase overflowing with plumes, flowers, and vines that draped down its sides. He pushed a spindly vine aside to spy on the widow without being seen.

"Hiding from a scorned woman?" Someone tapped him on the shoulder. "I would not be surprised to find that one or two will throw their drinks in your face tonight." The familiar singsong voice continued. "Ever the rogue, Evan Macleod, who are you hiding from today?"

"I was not aware you were to attend this ball." He turned, took the young woman's hand, and lifted it to his lips. While leaning over it, he looked up to meet Grant's sister's familiar green eyes.

His breath left, as he wasn't prepared for how much she had changed in the two years she'd been gone.

Felicity Murray had blossomed into a breathtaking beauty without compare. Despite knowing her for years, he would have been hard pressed to recognize her unless, like that moment, she'd spoken first.

Her face had lost its childish roundness and was now oval-shaped. Her lips remained plump, and her eyes, those entrancing bright green eyes, were accentuated with long, lush eyelashes.

Dressed in a spellbinding light-pale-green gown, raven black hair was pulled up into an elaborate hairstyle.

She was magnificent.

The beauty arched a brow. "Cat got your tongue?"

"I am busy," he managed. "I was not aware that you were in town. Grant did not say."

Sparing him a glance, she leaned forward to look and see what he could have been spying. Evan cursed inwardly, as the widow and her companions had yet to move.

"She is a good target for someone like you. However, I doubt Sorcha Robertson will give you the time of day."

Despite himself, he had to ask. "Why do you think that?"

Felicity's eyes sparkled with mirth. "Because everyone is aware of your reputation. The only way to gain her trust would be to visibly change something about yourself."

Just then a robust man he did not recognize neared. "Miss Murray," the man said with a gallant, overly done bow. "I beg the honor of a dance tonight." He glanced at Evan with a silent, *"Go away."*

"Have we met?" Evan said, lifting a brow.

"Harvey Lewiston," the man said, and then returned his attention promptly to Felicity, who'd yet to speak.

Evan knew of Lewiston, a man with a reputation for business dealings that were barely legal enough to keep him from prison. The man was short and heavyset. He had shrewd eyes, a thick neck, and heavy jowls, which made him seem older than his early forties.

"Miss Murray?" Lewiston's lips curved, showcasing crooked, yellowed teeth.

As if on cue, a waltz commenced. Felicity spun around and grabbed Evan's arm. "Perhaps later, Mister Lewiston. I have just promised Mister Macleod first and second dances."

She all but dragged him away, but not in the direction of where people had begun dancing. They went through an arched doorway to a room with beautifully framed oil landscapes on the walls.

"I can help you gain the widow's trust. But you must help me in return." Felicity paced, every so often looking toward the ballroom. "I will assist in your quest to get Sorcha Robertson's attention. In return…"

He crossed his arms. "I do not require your help."

The sooner he returned to the ballroom and his objective the better. He did not have time for a distraction. Despite finding Felicity to be astoundingly beautiful, he would never dare attempt to even pretend to court her.

Grant would not only kill him, but he'd draw and quarter him first.

"Enjoy your evening Felicity," he said, and headed back toward the crowded ballroom.

The music and conversations flowed toward him as he stood at an archway. Harvey Lewiston came to him. "Where is Miss Felicity?"

"She has an aversion to horrible breath and had to go for fresh air after speaking to you."

The man's face contorted. "Childish insults will not help you win in this, Evan Macleod. Your roughish reputation is against you."

Indeed, the man's breath was rather repugnant, making Evan wonder what he ate. "Rather a rogue than smelling like a rotting corpse."

At the comment, the man huffed and turned away. A few steps later, he blew into his hand and sniffed.

Evan chuckled.

"Mister Macleod, I am told you wished to speak to me." The woman's husky voice was as alluring as the lowcut bodice of her tangerine dress.

Sorcha Robertson gave him a questioning look. "Miss Murry stated that you were interested in the painting I did. As you may be aware, the ones hung in the hall are all for sale, to raise money for the local orphanage." She motioned to the room he'd just walked from.

Before he could consider how Felicity could have managed to not only get past him, but also speak to the widow, he turned his attention to the woman.

When she offered her hand, he took it and kissed it. "Indeed. You are very talented." He offered his arm. "Can you tell me about it?"

His mind raced with what to do. Without the funds to do more than look at the art piece, he could perhaps find a way to make it look as if he wished to purchase it, but not do so.

Allowing the woman to guide him, he kept an eye out to ensure neither Felicity nor the annoying Lewiston was about.

They stopped in front of an oversized framed art piece that, after a few moments, he decided was a depiction of a bouquet. Slashes of bright colors were accompanied with blobs that he supposed were as close to flowers as the artist could muster.

Evan blinked, scrambling for something kind to say. "Your grasp of color is astonishing."

The widow's lips curved, and she lifted a hand to her chest. "Thank you for saying that. I do love bright colors. They make me happy."

"If happiness is the goal, then you have accomplished it with this...piece."

The woman's eyes moistened. "You are ever so kind."

Just then the idiot Lewiston appeared, his eyes darting here and there in what Evan assumed was a search for Felicity, who was probably cowering in a closet by now.

He spoke in a loud voice. "Miss Murray was admiring this piece as well. She expressed how well it would go in her sitting room."

Like a moth to a flame, Lewiston materialized on the opposite side of Sorcha. "Is this your work?" he asked her, pointedly ignoring Evan.

"It is." Sorcha Robertson became animated at her art gathering so much attention. "I only completed it two days ago."

"I must have it," Lewiston announced. "Cost is no object."

"We will bid for it," Evan announced. "I have already expressed interest in it for my own home."

"I will assure you that it will be me who wins the painting in the end. It will be a gift for a dear friend."

Sorcha looked to Evan, her eyes wide. "You must get it. I would prefer you have it."

Leaning to her ear, he murmured, "If I were to lose, I would hope to get time with the artist as a consolation." With that, he strolled away, leaving the woman to suffer listening, and smelling, Lewiston's explanation of why he would win it.

⇸⟫⟪⇷

AS THE MUSIC piece ended, Evan spotted Grant escorting a young woman from the dance floor. He waited until his friend walked closer.

"Is that beauty to be your first target?" Evan asked.

Grant looked across the room. "No. Her mother is expecting courtship and marriage. Therefore, she is not to be my target. I danced with her because no one else was. Now she has a line of men vying for a dance."

"Ever the philanthropist," Evan said, noting that indeed the young woman was blushing prettily as several men circled.

Evan looked around the room. He would wait a while before approaching Sorcha again. "I was not aware your sister had returned."

"Yes, she has. Why?"

"Because she has already annoyed me. She stuck her pert little nose in my quest for the widow. Going so far as to tell the woman I was interested in a dreadful art piece she painted."

Grant laughed. "Sounds like my sister. Did it help?"

With a shrug, he had to admit that it did. "I suppose so."

The next musical piece began, and both watched as Grant's

sister partnered with someone and danced. Her face bright with excitement, she moved with grace to the music.

"There's Miles," Grant said, and they watched as their friend, dressed from head to toe in black, escorted a slender blonde to the dance floor.

"Do you suppose he could singularly afford to sponsor the ship?" Grant asked Evan. "Miles is wealthy, why did he not volunteer to do it?"

"I believe he will pay his portion and not more. He is responsible for handling his family's fortune. The portion that is his may be sizeable, but it is hard to tell."

Although Miles often footed the bill for their entertainment, it was rarely extravagant. Mostly he ensured there was delicious food, expensive whiskey, and the female companions were from a house of good standing.

The song ended and Felicity made a beeline for her brother. With flushed cheeks, she accepted a glass of punch from a passing tray.

"Do you plan to bid on any art, brother?" she asked Grant. "I have a piece I'd like to try for."

Grant gave his sister a bland look. "No, I do not plan to bid. I haven't the funds for such things."

"What about you, Evan?" Felicity gave him a perfectly feigned innocent look. "Are you to purchase the bright portrait you so admired?"

"Miss Felicity." Harvey Lewiston materialized, his gaze pinpointing Felicity before looking to Grant. "I have been in search of your beautiful sister in hopes she will honor me with a dance."

Felicity looked to Evan.

"She was just saying how much she loves this song," Evan said.

As the yellow-toothed man guided her away, Grant gave Evan a warning look. "If I were you, I'd keep my distance. My sister is quite adept at the art of revenge."

A group of women walked past, purposefully hesitating in

front of them. Each of them a debutante, none the kind either of them was interested in.

"I must admit. It has been a long time since I've seen so many beautiful women," Evan said while searching for his target. "It is unfortunate that I have little to offer."

Grant lifted a glass in salute and sauntered away. Past him, Evan spied a woman whom Grant often consorted with.

The woman was married to a much older lord, who despite failing health, attended every ball. Once he was parked along a wall with a blanket over his lap, his wife would enjoy the evening, rarely paying the man, who inevitably fell asleep, any mind.

At noting that Sorcha had made her way to one of the settees, he hurried there before another man got the chance.

"I am afraid I have bad news," Sorcha said when he approached.

Ensuring to meet her gaze, his never wandering, he asked. "Oh, what is it?"

Her plump lips pursed as she flattened her hand over the top of her breasts. A ploy to get his attention directly where she wished. "Since you did not return to place a second bid, you were outbid by Mister Lewiston."

"A pity," Evan said, allowing his gaze to travel from her eyes down to where her hand remained splayed. "I prefer the masterpiece before me to the art piece. Therefore, I am not as heartbroken as I would be if someone else had delivered the news."

The statement had its desired effect and she gasped. "Mister Macleod, you say the most flattering things."

"It is the truth."

It was obvious he had to do but one thing, insinuate an assignation and she would agree. However, he had to be patient with how to approach the woman.

"Mister Macleod..." she began.

"This dance?" he asked, proffering his arm.

With a surprised expression, she accepted and allowed him to guide her to the dance floor.

As they turned and face other people, Evan found himself face to face with Felicity. Her fiery gaze met his. "That dreadful man will not leave me be."

"What do you wish me to do about it?"

They turned away and circled again with their partners before stepping around to the opposite person.

"Get rid of him," Felicity spat. "You told him I wanted that art."

They turned and she glared at him before they had to return to their respective partners.

Evan turned to look and, sure enough, Felicity danced with Lewiston. He coughed to cover up a chuckle.

"Is something wrong?" Sorcha asked, her gaze on his face.

"Nothing. I am perfect." He gave her what he knew was a devilish smile and she blushed.

When he turned, Felicity was there again. "Dance with me after this," she whispered.

"No," Evan said. "Stop talking to me."

Thankfully, the song ended, and he guided Sorcha to a tall table where they could stand.

"I will get you something to drink."

"No thank you," Sorcha said quickly. "I prefer to speak with you."

This was the time to ensure to follow along, but in a way to not seem overly eager. "Of course."

"I require you to help me with something." Felicity appeared and gave Sorcha a wide-eyed look. "Mister Macleod has kindly offered to help me with something. I will return him to you shortly." She took him by the arm and practically dragged him toward the open doors that led to a balcony.

Felicity had just ruined a prime opportunity. Evan grit his back teeth. "Can you not get your brother, or Miles even, to rescue you? I am on the verge of…"

Felicity squeaked as if seeing a mouse, grabbed his face, and pulled him closer. Then to his astonishment, kissed him right on the lips.

The kiss was what he could only describe as hard, her mouth hitting his with so much force that their teeth clashed.

Hands splayed out to his sides, he was sure no one would ever consider the kiss to be an actual romantic interlude. When Felicity shoved him away and wiped her mouth with the back of her hand, a spectator would be even more convinced.

"Sorry. Eww," Felicity exclaimed, looking to the door, and then she smiled. "I think it worked."

"What worked? Get away from me before Grant cuts me through with a sword."

She fanned her face. "Goodness, what a night. I needed to get rid of that awful Mister Lewiston. I cannot find Grant anywhere."

"Well. Good. Then."

He took a step backward and hurried back into the ballroom.

Sorcha was dancing with an earl, who it was rumored had been her lover. She laughed at something he said, her head falling back.

His opportunity was gone.

"Champagne?" Holding two flutes, Felicity gave him an apologetic look. "Sorry about that. Lewiston was following me. And I had to help you. You were looking much too eager."

Evan let out a long breath. "I was not." He took the flute, wondering if he was indeed saved from himself.

CHAPTER THREE

"**Y**OU SEEM DIFFERENT this morning." Her lady's maid, Ana, studied her in the mirror. "Your eyes are bright and there is a glow about you."

Felicity leaned closer to look at herself. "I look the same. It could be I was so tired, I slept like the dead. Now I am well rested."

Ana held up a morning gown. The yellow dress had a modest neckline with embroidered tiny roses around it and the cuffs of the sleeves.

Once dressed, she descended the stairs only to falter at seeing a huge, wrapped package being accepted by the butler.

"What is it?" Her mother neared it and looked over her shoulder to Felicity. "Did you bid on something last night?"

"No, Mother, I did not. Perhaps Father?"

Her mother shook her head. "It is doubtful. After walking through, he pronounced every one of them to be horrid."

"It is addressed to you, Miss," the butler said.

"Me?" She hurried to it. "I did ask Grant to bid on one for me. I did not tell him which one, however."

Despite her father stating he preferred she not bring up Grant, Felicity often did.

"Unless things have changed, he hasn't the resources to purchase such extravagances." Her mother lifted the card that came with the piece and looked to her. "Ah."

"Ah? What do you mean ah?" Felicity took the card and her

empty stomach turned. "Oh no. We must return it at once."

"It states on the card that he will not accept it back, but wishes you to enjoy it." Her mother looked to the large parcel. "Can I see it?"

With care so that she could rewrap it, Felicity untied the string and pulled back the thick brown paper.

Both she and her mother gasped at the same time.

"That is the ugliest thing I've seen in a very long time," her mother said, a giggle escaping. "My goodness, why would he think you would like it?"

Felicity set her face in an attempt to hide the growing annoyance. "Because the hateful Evan Macleod told him I did."

⇸⇷

THE NEXT AFTERNOON, Felicity held a teacup to her lips, studying her best friend Hannah Kerr's face over the rim.

She and Hannah often visited in the late morning. They'd done so for years to discuss what they planned for the day and such. Today, they were at Hannah's home in the small sitting room.

"I am so annoyed with Evan Macleod I could spit."

Hannah's pretty face lit up. "I think he has taken notice of you, and you of him."

"What?" Felicity placed the cup down. "Did you not hear what I said? He is the reason I am the owner of the ugliest painting ever done."

"I must admit," Hannah started, "I wish to see it."

Making a face, she shuddered. "No, you absolutely do not."

Deciding to change the subject, she smiled widely. "You must accompany me to Sorcha Robertson's gala. It will be fun."

"I cannot possibly," Hannah said with sad sigh. "I haven't a new dress and have rotated the ones I have so many times, it is impossible to hide the fact."

Hannah's father owned a huge establishment that included a tea house on one end and several other businesses. When a fire burned the entire building to ashes, her family's money, which had been kept sadly in a metal box that proved not to be fire safe, burned along with it. The only thing that remained was a second small tea house that barely brought in any income.

Thankfully, Hannah's mother's small inheritance remained. Along with it, the money they had in the bank was enough to live off of, but not enough to rebuild their business or allow for any extravagances.

"I have an idea," Felicity exclaimed, and jumped to her feet. "We will sell the ugly painting and use the money to buy you a new dress."

"You cannot possibly. What if Lewiston finds out?" Hannah frowned. "If need be, I can borrow one of yours. I am sure you have one that hasn't been seen lately."

Felicity tapped her chin while thinking. "I did not wish to purchase too many new ballgowns. I only had two made, so I find that I will be rotating those I have as well. I do have an older one, a pale blue one, which will suit you."

Lowering back to her seat, she studied her friend. Hannah not only needed a new ballgown, but she also needed shoes and other accessories. "I really do wish to sell the painting."

"If you hate it that much, then fine, I will accompany you, but I refuse to take the money." Hannah looked around the room. "I wonder where my mother is off to."

Just then Hannah's mother entered with a tray of biscuits; the aroma of spices filled the air. "Look what I just made."

She placed the tray on the table between Felicity and Hannah, her face glowing with excitement at her creation.

They nibbled on the delicious bites while Felicity tried to find out what she could about her friend's need of attire.

Despite the hardships, Felicity admired the Kerr women's tenacity. Neither Hannah nor her mother allowed the circumstances to affect their cheerful nature.

A BELL RANG over the door the next day when Felicity and Hannah entered the antiquities shop where they would sell the atrocious painting.

Despite the rather unremarkable exterior, the interior was surprisingly welcoming. Every piece for sale was pristine and the displays alluring.

An older man appeared, his keen gaze landing on each of them. "May I be of assistance?"

Hannah, who'd accompanied her mother there when they'd sold many items, took the lead. "Good afternoon, Mr. Hollenbeck. My friend wishes to sell a one-of-a-kind painting. So many have commented on it that I assure you it will attract many a client to bid for it."

Mr. Hollenbeck turned his attention to Felicity, who met his gaze.

"I am in need of the wall space for a newly acquired piece," Felicity explained.

The man frowned. "Can you describe it?"

"It is a floral depiction against a study in color," Felicity said with a sigh, and then purposely hesitated. With a well-practiced frown, she met the man's eyes. "I am considering if indeed I should part with it. I do believe Duke Rosenthal showed a keen interest. I could contact him directly, couldn't I?" she asked Hannah, who nodded.

The man's expression softened, and his lips curved. "There is no need for you to go to all that trouble. I can have it picked up and ensure that the duke, as well as others, has the opportunity to see it."

"That would be lovely," Hannah said to Felicity. "Mr. Hollenbeck will ensure the painting finds the perfect owner."

The man offered them an amount, sight unseen, and they left with a bit more money than Felicity expected, but probably not as much Mr. Lewiston had paid for it.

"LET US ENJOY a dessert," Felicity said, and they ducked into an ice cream parlor. They ate while discussing what to do with their newly acquired funds.

"A most delightful way to spend the day," Hannah exclaimed as they walked out of the parlor.

Felicity hesitated, noticing that Evan stood across the street, looking dashing as he held the door of a jewelry shop open for a woman who hurried out and toward another shop.

Upon seeing them, he crossed the road.

"Good afternoon, ladies," he said, meeting first Hannah's gaze and then Felicity's. She frowned up at him. Not because it was unpleasant to see him, but because her stomach did funny things at his presence and she did not like it one bit.

"Did you purchase a bauble for a friend?" Felicity asked, looking past him to the jewelry store.

He smiled. "I did not find anything to my liking, I'm afraid."

When he fell instep alongside, Felicity decided to ask him about her brother. "I am convinced it is time for Grant to return home. You should help me convince him of it. It is past time he and Father make up."

"I am not sure I'm the best person to have that conversation with your brother. As you are aware, I too do not have a close relationship with my father at this time."

Felicity wanted to shake him. "That is because you are both stubborn as goats."

"I wasn't aware you have ever been in the presence of a goat." When his lips curved to show a flash of white, she let out a breath.

"There is no need for you to walk with us. We are almost to Hannah's home and I only live a block further."

"I could not possibly allow you to walk the rest of the way unescorted."

Hannah, ever so innocent, chose this time to assert her opinion. "I agree with Evan. Despite the early hour, you should be escorted. One never knows."

Letting out a calming breath, Felicity turned to her friend. "Will it not be worse to be seen walking with a well-known rogue than to walk unescorted?"

"I didn't think about that." Hannah looked to Evan and gave a soft shrug. "You do have such a reputation...which, of course, I do not believe to be true."

Evan let out a husky chuckle. "Thank you so much, Miss Hannah. You are a gem."

Her eyes rolled so hard Felicity got dizzy. "Hannah, do not be so naïve. Evan deserves every bit of that reputation. He is without a doubt every bit a scoundrel."

"You wound me," Evan said, looking anything but.

They continued walking after Hannah entered her house. Evan watched her go. "I wasn't aware that you and Hannah were such good friends."

"We are. She is a wonderful person."

"How is her family faring after what happened?"

Felicity didn't like discussing her friend, especially as she wasn't sure how much Evan knew. However, everyone was aware of what had happened to the Kerrs.

"They make do, I suppose. Despite it, Hannah is always in good spirits," Felicity said then looked up at him. "You would know what being a wastrel is like."

His jaw tightened. "I do know about making bad decisions. Mister Kerr's situation was not his fault. Thankfully, I do not have a family that depends on me."

Instantly, Felicity regretted her brash comment. "I should not have said that. I apologize. You shouldn't be made to pay with such rude comments for mistakes made when young."

He nodded. "Apology accepted."

Walking beside her, Evan seemed without a care. Conversation with him was fluid, and Felicity was curious to know more about him. Despite having known him for many years, it felt as if they'd grown into very different people than when they were young and their families visited often. When two women passed by, he placed a hand on her elbow and steered her around them, immediately removing it. There was something about Evan; the ease of being with him was natural, as if they'd had a close friendship.

"Why are you so interested in the widow?"

His right eyebrow lifted. "She is a beautiful woman."

The comment, although true, made her cringe. Evan was a single man without commitments and free to do as he chose. Therefore, she could not say that his reply was a lie. There was something he, her brother, and the other two rogues were plotting.

"I have one more question," Felicity began. "Are you and my brother planning to…"

"We have arrived," he interrupted, unnecessarily pointing to the front door.

"I am not finished." Felicity took a step closer and whispered. "Are the four of you planning a heist?"

"A what?" he replied with a chuckle. "What would we be taking?"

"You tell me." Giving him a pointed look, she waited.

Instead of a reply, he leaned closer and pressed a kiss to the tip of her nose. "Enjoy your day, Felicity."

Rounding her, he continued on his way, whistling.

After tracking him for a few moments, Felicity lifted her skirts and rushed up the stairs. The door opened before she could reach for the knob. Her father scowled down at her and then looked to where Evan turned the corner.

"Why were you walking alone with him?"

"Evan walked me from Hannah's house after we ran into him outside the ice cream parlor." She started to walk past, but her father cleared his throat.

Whenever he didn't believe someone, it was his custom to clear his throat and stare. Felicity turned to face him. "I am telling the truth, Da. Evan Macleod has absolutely no interest in pursuing me."

"Then why the kiss?"

It was her turn to frown. "To annoy me. He kissed my nose."

"Much too personal. That kind of display in the middle of the street where anyone could see."

"Father, why are you home?" Felicity asked, removing her shawl and placing it along with her reticule on a side table. "It is rather early."

"Do not change the subject, young lady."

Her mother appeared from the direction of the kitchen. "What happened? Hamish, why are you frowning at Felicity?"

"She allowed that scoundrel, Evan Macleod, to kiss her in front of the house. Outside..." he continued. "In the middle of the day."

"And in the middle of the street," Felicity added. "Apparently, Da thinks he is interested in me."

Her mother gave her a pointed look. "Missus Middleton told me that she thought to have seen you kiss Evan at the gala the other night. What exactly is going on, dear? You are aware of Evan's reputation."

She let out a sigh. "Very well. I did kiss Evan at the gala. But that was because that smelly Harvey Lewiston was following me."

There was a silent beat as her parents obviously scrambled with what to say.

It was her mother who spoke first. "That is not a way to act when out in public. I will speak to Evan myself and ensure he is aware you have no intention of any—"

"Courtship. You may never see him again," her father finished.

Felicity sighed. "I assure you, Da. Evan Macleod has no delusions of any kind of courtship between us."

Thankfully, her parents went to the other room to have tea and discuss whatever it was that had her father there during that time. They pointedly excluded her from accompanying them, which suited her fine as she wasn't sure when someone would show up for the painting.

"Miss Hannah is here to see you," the butler announced as her friend hurried in.

"Mother is meeting friends for tea, so I decided it was the perfect time to see the painting before it goes to the shop," Hannah said.

Felicity motioned for her friend to join her. "It is most distressing. Father is here and he can see out the window from the study. Surely, he will notice the carriage pulling up from the antiquities shop. Hopefully, he is too distracted with whatever he and Mother are discussing."

"Oh goodness," Hannah exclaimed. "Do you think he will mind you getting rid of it?"

"Doubtful. However, he is in a sour mood already."

She went on to explain to Hannah about Evan and the kiss. Despite the situation, both of them giggled while she talked.

Just then the butler went past the door, and they both held their breath and stared toward the doorway. It was but a few moments later that the most exasperating person entered without being announced.

"I am sorry to stop by without prior invitation, but I felt a need to see where the painting was hung." Harvey Lewiston's sharp gaze moved past them to where the item in question remained on the floor leaning against the wall.

"Oh," Felicity exclaimed. "We have not had the opportunity to hang it yet. It is hard to find the perfect spot." She nudged Hannah's foot with hers, hoping her friend could come up with something to say to send the man away.

"It may rain," Hannah said feebly, looking out the window. "If you have to be anywhere, you should hurry, Mister Lewiston."

Instead, he walked further into the room and peered out the window to a perfectly clear sky. "I am not bothered by a light drizzle."

The butler walked by again. He looked a bit haggard at this point. Moments later, he came to the doorway. "There is man here to pick up a painting. He asked for you, Miss Felicity."

"Oh." Felicity's stomach clenched. What horrible timing for Lewiston to have come by. She scrambled with what to do and how to handle it. When Gerard gave her a questioning look, her mouth opened. "Me?" The last thing she needed was for her mind to freeze, and the only instinct that seemed present was to run away and hide in her bed. Instead, she swallowed. "I-I am not..." She stopped speaking and lifted her gaze to Gerard, hoping he received the message to help her out of the situation.

"Should I send him away?" Gerard asked, looking straight at the wrapped portrait. "Or give them that?" He pointed to it.

"No!" she all but yelled. "Show him in."

A man wearing bright red suspenders and a hat that looked much too small for his head with an oversized handkerchief drooping from his front pocket appeared next and went straight for the still wrapped portrait.

Lewiston stepped in front of it. "What is the meaning of this?"

"That one," Felicity said, pointing to an oil painting of a floral bouquet that her mother loved.

The man looked at it and shrugged. He grabbed it, grunted at its weight, and managed to walk out with it just moments before her father walked in.

"What is with all the..." He stopped talking at seeing Lewiston. "Harvey, I was not aware you were here. I am glad you came. There is something we should discuss regarding the project you brought up the other day."

The men walked off, Lewiston seeming delighted to have her father's attention.

"What project could they possibly have together?" Felicity

asked, walking to the doorway.

The butler walked in and stared at the blank space. "Are you sure that was the painting they came for?"

Why Gerard took a sudden interest in what hung on the wall was beyond her. "Yes. It will be replaced with that one." She pointed to the wrapped one. Despite a questioning look, the butler was silent, for which she was grateful. The soft buzzing in her ears seemed to grow louder and she walked backward until she collapsed onto a settee.

"WHAT AM I going to do now?" Felicity asked when left alone again. "Do you think we can exchange it?"

Hannah shrugged. It was obvious she tried not to laugh. "Was the painting the man took instead valuable?"

"I have no idea. Come, let us go out into the garden. I need fresh air to consider what to do."

They remained for a bit and then Hannah announced she had to return home.

Upon entering the room, both froze.

"As soon as I found out that Felicity admired the piece, I acquired it for her. It is my hope that your daughter would accept this token of my esteem for her," Lewiston was explaining.

There were deep creases between her father's brows as he stared at the monstrosity that had been hung in place of the other one. "Felicity liked this?" Thankfully, he did not ask about the oil painting that had been removed.

Lewiston looked to Felicity. "I must admit that the reason for my visit was to ask that you do me the honor of attending the event at Sorcha Robertson's house this Friday."

"I-I," Felicity stuttered. "I am so sorry, but I've already accepted an invitation."

"From whom?" Her father asked, his eyes narrowing.

"Please do not say Evan." Her mother entered and lowered to a settee. Upon seeing the portrait on the wall, she practically leaped to her feet. "Felicity? Where is…" she began.

"I am so sorry," Felicity interrupted, avoiding her mother's gaze and looking from her father to Lewiston. "Evan Macleod asked me just earlier this afternoon and I said yes."

Her mother sighed loudly, and her father grunted.

Without looking at anyone, Felicity gathered her skirts. "Goodness, I totally forgot something. If you will excuse me. Good day, Mister Lewiston."

Thankfully, no one tried to stop her as she raced from the parlor, down the corridor, and up the stairs to her bedroom.

Panting heavily, she pushed her bedroom window open and leaned out, attempting to catch her breath.

Outside the window, Lewiston came into view. He hurried to his carriage and climbed inside.

Now she had to figure out how to explain the missing portrait to her mother, and somehow, she would exchange it with the dealer.

Lastly, she would have to inform Evan he was escorting her to an event at the house of the woman he was hoping to lure into whatever scheme he and her brother hatched up.

Returning to Glasgow was becoming a complicated affair.

CHAPTER FOUR

"**Y**OU DID WHAT?" Grant's loud laughter carried from the dining room to the study, where Evan did his best to concentrate on the ledgers. The small monthly stipend from his investments had arrived, and he tried to figure out how best to use the funds while somehow leaving enough for a new suit.

Deciding the old clothes would have to do, he pushed the book away and stood.

Just then a female voice sounded, her laughter entwining with Grant's. Had a woman spent the night? He'd not heard anything. Then again, he'd drunk quite a bit before going to bed and had slept soundly.

Intrigued at the idea of Grant hosting a woman for the night, which had never happened before, he went to investigate.

At the dining table square in the middle was a platter of sausages and bacon, and next to it a basket of what looked to be freshly baked scones. The aroma was intoxicating.

"Join us," Grant said, motioning to the food. "It is very delicious."

Felicity lifted a cup to her lips, her gaze traveling up his body. "You seem out of sorts."

"What is this?" he asked, motioning to the mountain of food. "Did you invite a platoon of soldiers for a meal?"

"It seems my sister is up to another of her games and made up a story to our mother that she was feeding street urchins. All this was done in order to get permission to leave the house and come here with an urgent matter." Grant began cutting into a rather plump sausage and Evan hurried to take a seat.

"Who cooked all of this?" Evan asked while piling food onto his plate.

Felicity finished chewing. "Mother, Cook, and I did."

"Why did you need to get out of the house?" Grant asked just as a woman came to the doorway. "Miss Felicity, we should head back."

It was Ana, Felicity's companion. Ana managed a soft smile at Grant. "Mister Grant, you are very much missed."

Grant stood, went to the woman, and kissed her cheek. "Thank you. I miss you all as well."

"I will only be a moment longer," Felicity said, reluctantly pushing her plate away. She then turned to Evan. "You must accompany me to the fete this Friday at Sorcha Robertson's house. Once we arrive, I will spend the evening with Hannah."

"Why does he have to escort you?" Grant gave Evan a pointed look. "Is there something I should know?" Grant was not as tall as him, but the man often trained with boxers, so Evan had no wish to get into a hand-to-hand battle with him.

He didn't dare meet his friend's glare. "Would you care to explain why I must escort you and not your brother, or your parents for that matter?"

"Because." She let out a long sigh. "I am trying to avoid accepting Harvey Lewiston's invitation. If I said to be attending with my brother or parents, or even Hannah for that matter, he would have insisted to accompany me. I know you do not have an invitation, and you wish to get to know that woman." She hesitated and looked to Grant. "I will find out what the lot of you is up to, by the way."

Grant studied him and then Felicity. "Why is Mother cross with you? You stated she was glad that you were doing this to redeem yourself."

"Ah yes." Felicity's cheeks turned bright pink. Evan had to admit she was quite a beauty, and despite her penchant for getting into strange situations, very enticing.

"I accidentally sold one of her favorite paintings. I meant to give them the monstrosity Mister Lewiston gifted me. Unfortunately, he was there when they came to pick it up."

Her gaze pinned him, and Evan's body instantly reacted. It was as if she touched him.

"It is your fault. All of it. Therefore, you will repay me by escorting me." She reached for the plate, lifted a piece of sausage, and bit it in half. Both he and Grant winced.

"It suits me perfectly, a way to get closer to the widow." When Grant gave him a pointed look, he added, "I wish to court her. She is quite alluring."

"You are indeed a rogue," Felicity said with a glare.

She then glanced at her brother. "I require your help in exchanging the portraits as well. This is partly your fault since you insist on keeping Evan as your friend."

With that, she whisked from the room, leaving a trail of a light citrus scent.

"She is the most annoying little minx," Grant said, refilling his plate. "This is too much food. I do feel guilty eating it."

Evan frowned in the direction where Felicity had gone. "I must admit, it is good luck that I will be going to the soiree tomorrow night. I must find a way to convince Sorcha Robertson to not only be my lover, but also finance the venture."

THAT NIGHT, EVAN entered the Walker's hotel lobby on Buchanan Street and walked to where men usually gathered. It was not as prestigious as being a member of a gentlemen's club, but those who did not wish to be members of a club or, like him, could not afford the dues, often relaxed at the Walker hotel, or other such places.

He found a seat at the long, pristine bar and ordered a whiskey. In a matter of minutes, Miles would appear, as it was their custom to meet there to discuss goings-on.

The lord entered, attracting the attention of everyone in the room. It was not just his exotic looks, but something about his friend commanded attention from both men and women.

Miles stood next to him. "Let us sit over there." He motioned to a lone table in the far corner of the room.

Once settled, his friend grimaced and stretched out his left leg, his right bent at the knee.

"What happened to your leg?" Evan asked.

"I fell," Miles said, his face stoic.

"Ha!" Evan exclaimed. "Were you climbing out of a window, perhaps?"

Miles fought to keep a straight face, therefore confirming what Evan had said. "She was well worth the risk."

Just then, a server appeared and placed two glasses on the table. "Anything else, my lord?" Miles shook his head.

"I have to ask," Evan started, "can you afford to sponsor the ship alone? If so, why are you not? You can be richer for it."

Miles shrugged. "I do not know the exact amount that is required. However, I prefer to enter into this sponsorship as a group and not front the entire amount. That way, we all win or lose equally."

Of course, if they used his money and lost it all, they would be hard-pressed to repay Miles. It was a smart strategy on his part.

"I understand. I would hope to be as intelligent as you once I recover some of my fortune."

Just then a familiar figure crossed the room toward them. Both he and Miles stood when Robert Macleod, Evan's father, neared. "Evan." His sharp gaze met his before moving to Miles. "My lord."

Despite having known Miles since youth, his father insisted on using titles.

"Would you like to join us?" Evan asked, genuinely glad to see his father. "How are you, Father?"

His father shook his head. "I was just leaving. There is much to do to prepare for your mother's birthday, do not forget. It is tonight." He hesitated and looked to Miles. "You are welcome as well, my lord."

"Of course I will be there," Evan said. "I look forward to spending time with the family."

There was a flicker of surprise in his father's face, and he nodded. "Very well then. Five o'clock sharp."

As he walked away, Evan let out a breath. "He will forever be disappointed in me."

Miles studied him for a short moment. "I think he only sees his son. How are the plans for your quest going?"

"Some progress. I must proceed with utter care if I do not wish for her to suspect anything," Evan said. "And you, what do you plan to do? Remember, you agreed to be part of this."

After a leisurely drink, Miles's lips curved. "Louisa Kent."

"What?" Evan let out a long soft whistle. "That will definitely be a challenge. She is not one to be toyed with." A rare beauty, after being widowed and left penniless, Louisa Kent had turned the town inside out by becoming a courtesan and often was seen with some of the most distinguished men in Scotland. It was rumored that despite receiving numerous marriage proposals, she never accepted, preferring her independence.

Now, very wealthy, thanks to her benefactors, she had no reason to do more than enjoy her life.

"I like a challenge," Miles said, meeting his gaze. "If I am able to gather the amount necessary for my portion of the sponsorship from her, it will be…"

"A miracle?" Evan interjected. "An impossibility. No, perhaps a crazy delusion on your part."

A chuckle displayed Miles's deep dimples. "Ah, so you have little faith in my prowess. I will prove you wrong."

HIS MOTHER'S BIRTHDAY fete at the Macleod estate was a bigger affair than Evan expected. There were three other families in attendance, including Hannah's and Grant's. When he, Miles, and Henry entered the room, they were greeted warmly. Grant had opted not to attend, citing another gathering he'd promised to be present for.

"What did you get mother?" his older brother, Richard, asked.

"Earrings," Evan replied with a bored expression. "Why do you ask?"

His brother, ever the protector, shrugged. "I was prepared to say that my gift was from the both of us."

Evan studied his brother, who was five years older. Richard had always been the responsible one, working with his father to ensure the family's shipping company continued being successful. Part of what made him equally aggravating, and admired by Evan, was his penchant for selflessness.

"Thank you."

His brother smiled at him and gave him a side hug. "It is nice to have you here."

Despite sitting across the table from Felicity, she ignored him, preferring to keep a running conversation with her friend, Hannah.

"I have not seen you much the last couple days," Evan said to Henry. "Working hard for the investment?"

His friend's lips lifted at the corners, but he did not respond as Hannah chose that moment to look across the table at Henry. Their gazes locked for but an instant, but it was enough for Evan to note there was something there.

"Penniless," he whispered.

"I am aware," Henry replied. "Now to your question. Yes, I am almost certain to be fully funded well before the deadline."

"That is good news. My efforts, however, are proceeding slowly."

"A toast," his father announced, and began to speak about his mother. The words flowed over Evan as the professions of admiration and love continued. His mother's eyes misted and she wiped at the corners with a dainty handkerchief, her face aglow with love.

Evan met his mother's gaze and smiled at her, noting how her expression softened. When he finally glanced away and across the table, Felicity studied him with a quizzical look.

Tearing his eyes from hers, he looked back to his father, who concluded by wishing his wife a happy birthday and everyone joined in.

The love between his parents was palpable. Something he wished for one day. However, due to his present financial circumstance, he could never aspire to a wife. He could barely afford to support himself as things stood.

A rush of something akin to fire traveled up his spine and he straightened in his chair. Once they came up with the money to sponsor the ship, he would be in a perfect position to seek a wife.

He dared a glance toward Felicity.

Not her, of course. Then again, she'd become a beautiful woman, who was intelligent and quite adept at most everything that was required in a wife. At the direction of his thoughts, Evan shook his head. For some inexplicable reason, for the first time, whenever he thought of a woman, he felt lighter, as if the world became a brighter, more interesting place.

Utter foolishness, he chided himself internally. Felicity was his friend's sister, and whatever he felt was nothing more than a passing fancy.

Besides, Felicity was well aware of what he did, his plan to seduce Sorcha Robertson. A woman like her would never accept a proposal of courtship from a rogue like him.

FRIDAY ARRIVED, THE sunny day blending into a beautiful evening with just enough breeze to allow one to wear a light coat, or wrap for the women, comfortably.

The carriage came to a stop in front of the Murrays' home, and Evan looked across at Grant, who visibly stiffened.

"When will you give in and have a frank talk with your father?"

His friend shook his head and looked toward the house. "I imagine we will clear things up sooner or later. However, he is stubborn and refuses to meet with me...unless I agree to certain terms."

"Ah," Evan said, not adding that Grant was as headstrong as his sire. "Will you do me the favor of retrieving your sister? I do not wish to be punched in the face by the stubborn man."

"Of course," his friend replied, his jaw visibly tight.

When Grant reached the door, it was opened by the austere butler, whose face immediately transformed at seeing Grant. The man patted Grant's shoulder and opened the door wider so that Felicity could walk out.

He'd expected her to look beautiful, and yet, he was unable to keep from gawking.

Emerging in a gown with a short-sleeved blue bodice and cream-colored skirts, she was stunning. Her dark tresses were swept up into a simple but flattering style that framed her face perfectly. She wore a small tiara, or something of the sort, that was tucked into her hair so that it was just visible. It was so like her to add certain touches that were not overtly obvious and yet delightful.

She wore gloves that went to her elbows, and as she walked out, Felicity handed her brother a shawl that he placed over her shoulders. When she smiled at Grant, deep dimples formed in her cheeks, and without expecting it, Evan smiled as well.

Clearing his throat, he leaned back into the seat when she looked toward the carriage. He had to maintain an aloof demeanor. It would not do to show any interest in his closest friend's sister.

Not only was she forbidden fruit for a rogue like him, but anyone who dared court Felicity would do so acknowledging it would lead to marriage.

Her father had been right to be angry that he'd walked her home. Any assignation with him could ruin any chances of a good match for the beauty.

When she entered the carriage, her gaze met his and she giggled. "Aren't you a picture?" she exclaimed.

"Of what?" Evan didn't mean to, but his voice held an irritated tone.

"Of handsomeness," she replied, leaning forward and giving him a pointed look. "The color of your jacket, it suits you."

He looked to Grant who, used to their repartee, ignored them, and was currently peering out toward the house, a sullen expression marring his face.

"Umm," Evan stumbled on how to return the compliment. "You look festive."

"Thank you," she replied, and lifted a gloved hand to pat her hair. "Mother insisted on the tiara. A bit much."

"Are your parents attending?" Evan asked, which made Grant finally look at his sister.

"No. They were, but Mother has a headache." She lifted a slim shoulder, immediately drawing his attention to the expanse of skin exposed by the cut of the bodice. The front of her gown was not as low cut as most women wore, which made Felicity even more alluring.

And yet, the hint of the top of her breasts that lifted and lowered with each breath affected him more than a fully unclad woman's body.

It took monumental effort to drag his gaze away and look out to the passing scenery.

"How far is this blasted place?" he mumbled.

Felicity rolled her eyes. "This is a delightful ride. Whatever is wrong with you?" She looked to him and then to Grant. "Both of you act as if headed for the gallows. If your plan is to gain the attention of women, it will not work if you walk in with those glum expressions."

"We do not have any plan," Grant said, finally smiling. "Your meddlesome nature makes you come up with plots that do not exist."

"Hmm," she said, sliding a look to Evan. "I have a plan. To enjoy the evening to its fullest, and since Mother is not here, she has requested that you remain by my side at all times." She gave her brother a triumphant look. "Promise."

Grant let out a breath. "I will be beside you the entire time. I must keep unsuitables away."

When she giggled, it was a melodious sound. "Goodness, Grant, I cannot wait to see who you consider suitable. Do not forget that I do wish to dance."

"You can dance with Evan."

Her gaze slowly lifted to meet Evan's, and he let out an involuntary breath and swallowed.

"Perhaps one dance; let us not forget, brother, that Mister Macleod is here for the sole purpose of gaining Sorcha Robertson's attention."

Grant nodded and looked at him. "He can do both. Evan has many talents."

"What of you, brother?" Felicity asked, studying Grant's face. "Who are you hoping to get to know better?"

Grant motioned out the window. "We arrive."

They waited in the queue of carriages for their turn. Evan studied Felicity, whose eyes twinkled with excitement.

"You love these social events." It was a statement, not so much a question.

She nodded, her fingers tapping with impatience on the seat. "I do. After the very long, dreary winter, I look forward to the Season. It is quite fun to see the new lovely gowns everyone is wearing."

"How many new gowns did you have made?" Grant asked, giving her a playful look.

"Just two. It feels wasteful to have more made since I have so many from previous years. No one will remember each one of them."

When the carriage moved up, she grinned, but then blew out a breath when, again, it stopped before reaching the front of the home.

Evan was keenly aware of where Sorcha lived. The grand house had been left to her by her not-so-recently departed husband, along with a sizeable fortune. There were speculations that he'd left large sums to other women, whom he'd maintained assignations with, but it did not diminish the fact Sorcha was a very wealthy woman.

They finally reached the front of the queue, and the door to the carriage was opened by a footman, who placed a wooden stool at the bottom of the carriage steps. Grant alighted first and assisted Felicity.

When Evan stepped down, he considered whether or not to hold out his arm for her. Thankfully, Grant saved him by doing so.

With her on her brother's arm and him on the opposite side, it would look to observers as if he was merely accompanying them. No tongues would wag, linking him to her.

It was well known, after all, that he and Grant were childhood friends.

Sorcha's house was resplendent. Chandeliers laden with freshly cleaned crystals reflected the light of the candles, making the rooms bright and welcoming.

Huge paintings with slashes of colors hung from most walls, the familiar style making Evan look to Felicity, who pointedly stared at a particularly garish one.

"I hear you are enamored with that style of art," he murmured into her ear, earning a sharp glare.

Just then, dressed in a color he could only describe as apple green, Sorcha approached. From her ears and throat, light green gemstones sparkled with each movement. Her hair was curled and pinned to within an inch of its life. The intricate style did not move one bit as she whirled around to face him and his companions.

"Evan, darling," she cooed, her gaze locked to his. Upon nearing, she turned to Grant and Felicity barely for a second before looking to him again.

In her swift scan, her eyes landed on Felicity's hand on her brother's arm. Her lips curved just a bit.

"I am so glad you came," Sorcha said to Felicity. "Please, go and mingle."

Upon the obvious dismissal, Felicity's face hardened, her sharp eyes moving from him to the widow. "It is lovely to see you as well, Mrs. Robertson."

In that moment, Evan couldn't help but compare the two women. They were as different as night and day. Although both beauties, there was a freshness and calmness about Felicity. Not only that, but where Sorcha gave the impression of experience and secrecy, Felicity exuded a quiet strength and allure.

Sorcha leaned forward and flattened her hand on his chest. "We barely had time to talk last time I saw you. Now I'm hosting; therefore, I am not sure how I could possibly have time."

He took the bait. "Afterwards, you will probably be exhausted. Therefore, we will have to leave it for another day." He lifted her hand and kissed the back of it.

After presenting his arm, he guided the woman to where others were arriving. It looked as if every prominent family in Glasgow was represented. He wondered if his parents would be there.

"Mrs. Robertson, were my parents invited?"

Disengaging from an overly made-up woman, Sorcha turned to him. "Yes, of course." She scanned the room. "I believe they arrived a few moments before you did."

His stomach lurched; he would have to make sure his parents did not try to meddle at seeing him accompanying the widow. His mother would be alarmed if he did not pursue someone other than a young woman who would bear her grandchildren.

Sorcha went about her hosting responsibilities after insisting he find her for a dance, and he in turn went in search of Grant.

THE EVENING WAS in full swing. Evan had managed to dance with Sorcha and avoid his parents. Upon catching sight of his father, he dipped out to the garden.

Like the rest of the house, the garden was perfectly maintained and overly decorated. Lanterns lit narrow pathways, inviting one to wander forward.

At the sound of footsteps, Evan turned just as a woman rammed into his chest.

"Ouch," Felicity exclaimed. Then she looked up at him, her eyes widening. "Oh, it's you."

"Sorry to disappoint…"

She grabbed his arm and pulled him off the path. "Shhh."

Just then, Harvey Lewiston hurried past, his arms pumping in his effort to go faster.

"What are you doing?" Evan whispered.

"That man is intent on following me."

Evan let out a breath and turned to find where Lewiston had gone. He took a couple steps and turned back to face Felicity. "Do you not have other suitors?"

She gave him a bland look. "I just returned from Edinburgh, barely had time to meet anyone."

"There is that." Unsure why, he took a step closer. "You should ensure to find a willing suitor to keep people like Lewiston at bay."

"Are you volunteering?" Her gaze flickered over his face.

He wasn't sure, but almost certain she teased.

"I could, I suppose," Evan said, sliding his fingers up the side of her face and gently lifting it. He meant it as a jest, but something in his chest fluttered.

Leaning forward, he took her mouth. It was a gentle kiss. At least, at first it was. Just a press of his lips against hers.

When she returned the kiss, the ground seemed to shift and he wrapped his arms around her. Felicity fell against him, giving into the moment. His head spun at the perfect fit between them. How would he keep from this woman after this? Trailing his lips to the edge of hers, he began to move down the side of her neck.

Something bit his leg, perhaps a dog, and he straightened, realizing it was possible to be seen.

When Felicity pushed at his chest with both hands, he realized she'd kicked him. Especially when she started hopping on one foot. "Ouch," she exclaimed.

"Why did you kick me?" he hissed.

"Why did you kiss me like that?" she replied with a glare. "You should not have done it."

"I agree."

At his statement, she blew out a breath and turned away. "You hurt my toes." Wincing, she hobbled toward the main pathway. "Do not follow me."

"I should carry you." Before she could respond, he swept her up in his arms. "I will take you to Grant."

She pushed at his chest. "Put me down. If we are seen, we will have to explain what you and I are doing alone here in the garden."

Voices approached, and he noted that Sorcha and several women walked in their direction. Just as the group turned, he tossed Felicity into a cluster of bushes.

"Mister Macleod," Sorcha said, meeting his gaze when he walked closer, doing his best to block their view of the bushes. "Whatever are you doing here alone, away from the festivities?" She met his gaze and then searched the area behind him. "No assignation, I hope?"

"Of course not," he said, straining to hear sounds from the bushes.

Just then Lewiston returned. "Good evening, ladies." He managed to inch closer. "If you would like, I would be happy to escort you about. One never knows who could be out here alone."

Evan gave him a droll look. "There are rumors of wee trolls about in the bushes."

CHAPTER FIVE

"**W**HERE HAVE YOU been? I have the juiciest thing to tell you," Hannah exclaimed upon meeting Felicity near the powder room. She leaned closer to study her. "Your hairstyle has changed."

"That is because I was thrown into bushes by a brute," Felicity whispered. "I will never speak to Evan Macleod again."

She'd remained in the bushes, doing her best to keep from screaming with fright while the Evan held court with Sorcha and her prattling group. Then, to her utter chagrin, Harvey Lewiston had appeared and extended the conversation.

"Oh no," Hannah exclaimed. "I will speak to him and ensure he is aware it is most unacceptable to have treated you in such a manner."

Hannah's cheeks had pinked with exasperation. "Why did he throw you into the bushes?"

Rather than reply, Felicity took her hand and guided her toward the large ballroom. "We have more important matters to see to."

"Such as?" Hannah looked out, no doubt searching for Evan.

"My tiara. It must still be in the bushes."

When her friend turned to her, she let out a long breath. "I agree to help you look for it, but you must inform me immediately of what exactly occurred."

When the Macleods came into view, Felicity turned away, took two steps, and bumped into a man. When she looked up, it was obvious he was not happy by the crinkle of his brow.

"I apologize, sir. So very sorry."

His lips curved and he nodded. "I do not mind; it gives me an opportunity to introduce myself." The man was tall with a slender build. Well-dressed, his hair was longer than fashionable, but it suited him. By his strong burr, he was from the Highlands. And she had to admit, he was attractive.

"I am Calum Ross," he said, taking her hand. "Returned just recently from Inverness."

"I am Felicity Murray." She motioned to Hannah. "This is my dearest friend, Hannah Kerr."

While Calum greeted Hannah, Felicity caught sight of Evan, who in turn studied them with narrowed eyes.

"Mister Ross, have we met before?" Felicity asked.

He shook his head. "No, this is my first time here in Glasgow."

"Very nice to meet you. If you will please excuse us, Hannah and I have a pressing matter." Felicity smiled and tugged Hannah, who seemed to have lost her ability to speak. Her friend's attention was taken by someone on the dance floor.

They hurried around the side of the room until reaching the open doors to the garden. Stopping to catch their breaths, Hannah turned to peer back inside.

"Whatever are you looking at?" Felicity asked, looking in the same direction. "Is something wrong?"

"Henry Campbell is dancing with a young woman who looks enthralled."

"What?" Felicity looked over and, sure enough, the handsome Campbell guided one of the debutantes, who was definitely very beautiful and had garnered much attention. With his last name, he was the target of many prominent families for a good match. "I find it interesting that the four scoundrels are suddenly interested in women. They are up to something."

Once descending the gardens, Felicity went to the place where she'd been thrown into and bent at the waist to peer into the darkness. "We should have brought a lantern or something of the sort."

"A torch perhaps," Hannah replied dryly. "That would not have brought attention in the least." She moved a branch and peered down. "I see something."

"Ladies."

The voice made Felicity grind her teeth. "What do you want, Evan? Please go and leave us be."

"I came to help."

Too angry to keep her voice down, she whirled to face him. "It is your fault my tiara is in the bushes."

"Oh!" A couple who was walking by stopped and gawked. The woman, a well-known gossip, studied their faces. "Can we do something to help?" she asked, looking between the three, attempting to figure out who had been Evan's victim.

"No, thank you," Hannah replied. "I see it. Mister Macleod thought to have seen an insect land on the tiara and was overzealous in his quest to hit it."

The woman waited, still trying to figure out who had been wearing the tiara. When no one moved, the man urged her forward and they continued on their walk.

"You should keep your voice down," Evan told her then reached into the bushes and retrieved the sparkling item.

When she took it, he nodded and walked away, but not in the direction of the house.

Hannah let out a sigh. "When are you going to admit to being smitten with him? It is obvious he is with you."

"Nonsense," Felicity said, plopping the tiara on her head. "This is turning out to be the most overwhelming evening."

When they returned to the large ballroom, Grant neared and stood at her right. "You should be mingling more."

"I find myself in the mood for a good book and a cup of tea rather than being here." She gave him a pointed look. "You were supposed to remain with me, and yet this is the first time you appear. I've had to fight off that infuriating Mister Lewiston."

Her brother scanned the room for a long moment. "Would either of you like something to drink?"

Both she and Hannah shook their heads. Two men approached and asked them to dance, and they accepted. Admittedly, the music was lovely and the room not too overcrowded as some events tended to be, so it was a comfortable setting.

As she followed the steps to the dance, she caught sight of Evan also, dancing with the hostess. His gaze never left his partner's, which made Sorcha beam.

Seeming to sense her regard, Evan's gaze moved from his partner to meet Felicity's, and there was a hint of a smile at the corner of his lips. Felicity looked away, pretending not to have noticed.

She accepted another dance request and allowed the gentleman to escort her to the dance floor. Once they began the familiar twirls, her mind immediately returned to Evan.

Why had he kissed her in such a way? It was clear he was enamored with Sorcha Robertson. Although Felicity tried to convince herself that the reason he was wooing the woman was due to some kind of scheme, it was obvious, by the way he looked at her, Evan was in love.

Her breath caught and she stumbled. Thankfully, her partner was quick and caught her before she fell to the ground.

"Are you unwell?" he asked into her ear.

It seemed no one had noticed and she shook her head, concentrating to ensure to keep with the music. The tune, although lively, was no longer appealing as she realized how sad she was at the idea that perhaps Evan would marry Sorcha.

The fact who he married had nothing to do with her was of no consequence. Felicity was sure it would not end well.

Thankfully, the song ended, and she was escorted back to Grant. Her brother gave her a quizzical look. "Why do you look as if someone kicked your dog?"

"I do not have a dog." Felicity managed a bright smile. "As I said, I am not in the mood to be here."

Grant studied her. "Did you do something different? Your hair…"

"Let's dance." Felicity grabbed his arm and tugged him forward as a new song began. This time, it was a waltz. The last thing she wanted was to dance a waltz with her brother, but it seemed too late to retract.

Her brother was distracted, looking across the room at an older woman. Probably one of his benefactors. "Not now," he murmured giving her a distracted look. "I must speak to someone before the evening ends.

"Will you dance with my sister?" Grant asked Evan, who headed past them.

"Of course," Evan replied, his gaze clashing with hers. He took her hand and placed it onto the crook of his arm. Tingles of awareness traveled through her and her breathing hitched. However would she be able to dance with him? As it was, it was proving hard to breathe normally.

Leading her forward then placing one hand just behind her shoulder and extending the other, they began circling to the music.

The song flowed over them, seeming to enclose them in a world of their own.

When Felicity looked up into his eyes, her breath caught at the intensity with which he looked at her. His gaze darkened to the point his eyes became stormy.

Around and around they went. It was as if she floated above the ground, her feet barely touching the pristine marble floors. Her slippers soundlessly glided as he led them into larger circles and the other dancers melded into a mosaic of movement and color.

Not a word was spoken between them because there was no need. Whatever it was that happened between them could not be put into words. Or described, for that matter. It was as if their most inner beings communicated and agreed to become one.

Felicity gasped and managed to look away, but only for a moment before she had to meet Evan's gaze once again.

This time, his expression softened, his gaze lightening. He released the hold on her back, and she whirled away and then lowered to a curtsey while he bowed as the song ended.

The magic between them was instantly broken, like an abrupt waking from a deep slumber, when Sorcha waited for Evan on the side of the dance floor.

"I feel a need for fresh air," she exclaimed, fanning her face. "Would you be gracious enough to accompany me?" The woman did not grant Felicity even a glance as they walked away.

Felicity's eyes glazed over, and she blinked, doing her best to dispel the stupid tears that threatened to spill. More than anything, she was angry that she'd read so much into a simple dance.

Upon nearing Grant and Hannah, she could barely stand remaining there. "We should go."

She continued forward past people who gave her curious looks. Perhaps her expression was too telling of someone who'd been upset by something. It mattered little to her what people thought. All Felicity knew was that it was best to leave and avoid Evan Macleod at all costs.

Surely it would not be long before whatever she was feeling went away.

In the carriage, both Grant and Hannah did not ask her anything. She caught them exchanging questioning looks.

Finally, her brother, who had a curious nature, tapped her arm. "Did Evan say something to upset you?"

Startled at his question, Felicity realized that her actions after the dance would bring such conclusions. "No, he did not speak to me at all."

"Then why do you look as if heartbroken?"

At the question, Felicity managed a bark of laughter. "Why would I be heartbroken? I am not interested in any gentleman at this time."

When Grant looked to Hannah, Felicity could feel her best friend's study of her. If anyone suspected that she'd allowed her feelings free rein when it came to Evan Macleod, it was Hannah.

"What I think," Hannah began, "is that Felicity has not been courted properly. Although she has many friends, there has not been anyone calling on her other than Mister Lewiston."

"Ah," Grant replied, seeming satisfied. "Perhaps our parents need to see to a gathering to ensure it is made obvious that it is time for you to settle."

"Settle?" Felicity met her brother's gaze. "Is that what we do, brother? Do we settle for someone merely because it is time to marry?"

Grant let out a breath. "You would be the one to make the choice, of course. Our parents have always made it clear they do not wish to play matchmakers. Thankfully, social status isn't a factor for our family. Father is well-regarded and you will never lack for social invitations."

It was true and probably the reason that, at almost twenty, she remained unmarried. She'd enjoyed traveling and studying, loving the freedom of not being encumbered by marriage and children. Now, however, it was obviously all to change. Not only were her emotions changing, but just the thought of a child made her entire being tremble with want.

"You are right. It is time for me to settle."

"Perhaps we should come up with a better word," Hannah quipped. "How about 'marry'?"

Grant turned his attention to her friend. "What about you, Hannah?

"I do wish to marry, have for a while. However, the unfortunate episode that happened to my family brought my aspirations to a halt."

Her heart broke for Hannah, who'd been courted by a lord. The scoundrel had withdrawn his proposal immediately after finding out about the Kerrs' ruin. It turned out the man was virtually penniless and had hoped to garner a better life through

Hannah's dowry.

"Perhaps you and I can be celebrated together," Felicity exclaimed. "We must speak to our mothers about it."

"I am glad to see the frown replaced with excitement," Grant said. Although he meant well, the reminder of why she'd been upset felt like a punch to the chest.

Evan Macleod would never be hers. It was silly to have had such thoughts. She would meet someone else, be courted, and marry.

All thoughts of Evan had to be locked away, the key tossed.

CHAPTER SIX

T HE EVENING HAD become colder. It was early spring, and therefore, the warmth of the day quickly dissipated once the sun set.

"I find it interesting that you and I have never had the opportunity to get to know each other," Sorcha remarked, her gaze slowly climbing from his chest to hesitate on his lips, and then finally rising to meet his gaze.

"A crime," Evan replied, and took her hand to lift to his lips. The movements felt mechanical, without substance, and he had to concentrate to keep from comparing the woman before him to the one he'd held just minutes earlier on the dance floor.

Interesting that both women had green eyes. Sorcha's were gold-speckled and dark, while Felicity's were a delightful bright green. While Sorcha's lips were well-formed, they held no comparison to Felicity's plump pink ones that curved up at the edges. Her expressions always made people smile, as she was playful and easy to like. Easy to become infatuated with.

"You look at me as if you are guarding a very pleasant secret," Sorcha said, instantly taking Evan from his revelry.

"Should we continue our walk?"

Instead of turning to stroll, Sorcha lifted her arms and wrapped them around his neck, bringing him down for a kiss. Evan kissed her back, his body remaining disconnected.

The woman murmured, oblivious to the battle that raged in him. There was no comparison between this kiss as to what he'd felt when kissing Felicity. With Felicity, his entire being had reacted. Now with Sorcha, it was more numbness that came over him.

"Darling," Sorcha murmured. "Stay the night."

"I AM PLANNING a trip to Spain; you should consider coming with me." Sorcha looked to him from the bed the following morning as Evan hurriedly dressed.

"Enticing offer. I have some business dealings that demand I remain here for a time." Evan delivered the first hint to what would hopefully bring forth an offer of money. He had to act the part of not wishing for anything from Sorcha. "However," he continued, "I will try to make haste and hopefully can do so."

The fact he was in a hurry to leave that morning was not so much acting as it was that he could not stand to remain in the cloyingly perfumed room any longer. That and the fact he was not sure he would be able to continue the farce. Remaining with little money was not as daunting a task as it would be to continue to pretend to care for a woman who obviously expected men to do her bidding.

"Be a dear and pour my tea," Sorcha called out. She slipped from the bed, her nakedness, although admittedly attractive, not enticing him at the moment.

However, as she expected it, he ensured to take her in, his gaze roaming over her and hesitating at the patch of hair between her legs. When he met her gaze, she smiled.

"We can always return to bed," she purred.

"There is much for me to do, although the offer is very, very tempting." He pulled his coat on, ignoring her request to pour tea. Nearing her, he pressed a lingering kiss to her lips and then gave her what he knew would come across as a promising look. "Thank you. I never imagined something like this." He slid a look to the bed.

Delighted at his words, Sorcha placed a hand on his forearm. "Think about my offer."

Evan nodded and saw himself out.

OUTSIDE, THE MORNING was crisp and he pulled his scarf around his neck. Since the carriage had been taken by Grant the night before, he had to maneuver his way home on foot, or hail one for hire.

Needing to clear his head, Evan decided to walk for a while. He had to focus on the prize. In his estimation, another night or two and Sorcha would offer him anything to remain with her. It was then he'd make himself scarce, claiming to have to work to come up with the quantity needed for his portion of the sponsorship money.

A carriage slowed and then came to a stop. His brother's face appeared through the door. "Are you headed home?"

Evan got in and sat across from Richard. "I needed a walk to clear my head about certain things."

His brother gave him a questioning look. "You are quite far from home."

It was obvious he expected a response. Never keeping secrets between them until his financial fall, Evan wanted nothing more at the moment than to be able to share what he was doing with his brother.

"I spent the night with Sorcha Robertson." He waited for Richard's disapproval.

"You should tread with care. She is not one to be toyed with."

His brother's reply was unexpected, and also perhaps true. "Why do you say that?"

Richard frowned. "An acquaintance of mine grew to know her very well. He claims that when crossed, Sorcha can be very vindictive."

"What did she do?" Evan became wary. He had to proceed carefully so as not to bring out the ire of a woman who had as much money as Sorcha and could hire people to do her bidding. The carriage wheels on the right dipped into a rivet and they were jarred sideways before continuing.

"He said that she hired men to beat him. The poor dolt ended up in the hospital for weeks."

Evan swallowed. "I will have to take care then."

As they approached the estate, his brother peered out the window. "The old beauty remains as such," he said almost to himself.

"You should come inside," Evan said.

"No, I have early matters to see to. Perhaps soon."

Meeting his brother's gaze, warmth filled him. "Thank you."

It was eerily quiet when Evan walked into his home. No one greeted him at the door, and he wondered if his hired help had finally had enough and left.

"Mister Macleod." Norman appeared, his craggy face breaking into a smile. "There is a matter in the dining room that demands your attention."

He was not in the mood for another leaking roof, or floor in need of repair. However, ignoring what happened was not going to help either.

"I will be there shortly," he replied, removing his coat and scarf. Once the items were hung over the back of a chair, he took a breath and walked to the dining room.

"Surprise!" A chorus of voices made him take a step backward. "Happy birthday, dear lad," his mother exclaimed, hurrying to him and pressing a kiss to his cheek.

His father, more reserved, neared and patted his shoulder. "Happy birthday, Evan."

"Why do you catch me unaware every single year?" he asked, genuinely happy to see everyone. It was then he noticed Richard was there as well. He must have rounded the house and entered through the kitchen.

On the table was a fruit torte, as well as a spread of his favorite breakfast foods. It had been a family tradition to have a festive breakfast for him and his brother.

Evan had totally forgotten it was his birthday, and now he was glad to have gotten up so early to head home.

It was almost as if all the bottled-up heaviness was removed from him in that moment, and he almost melted against his brother when he came forward and hugged him. "I am glad to have been late and collected you," Richard whispered.

Grant descended the stairs and joined them as they all sat to eat. It was delightful to hear the lively conversation around the table as they chatted about this and that. As per usual, the discussion of past birthdays surfaced, and soon they laughed as the different antics of his childhood were brought up.

It was hard to not blurt out that he wished for nothing more than for more mornings like that.

While they shared the torte and their teacups were refilled, his mother placed a box in front of him. "From your father and me."

His father met his gaze and winked, letting him know he had no idea what was in the box.

It was a beautifully crafted pair of gloves and a scarf. "They are just perfect. I needed them very much."

His brother gifted him a new pair of riding boots, and he was also gifted embroidered handkerchiefs from the Macleod staff.

The meal ended much too soon, as everyone had to see to their daily duties. His father and brother to the business and his mother to whatever her social obligations were that day.

"Mother," Evan asked before they left. "Are you friendly with Missus Murray?"

"Yes," his mother exclaimed. "I will be seeing her today actually at a tea. Why do you ask?"

He looked over to ensure Grant did not overhear. "Will you inquire about Felicity? I heard she left Sorcha Robertson's home in a state last night."

His mother gave him a quizzical look and then glanced toward Grant. "He should see about his sister and family, not rely on others. I sincerely do not understand either you or his stubbornness when it comes to family." Pressing a kiss to his cheek, she allowed him to help with her cloak. "I will inquire and send you word."

"Thank you."

He walked his parents to the front door and once again hugged his mother. Just as his father left, he handed him an envelope. "See about all the repairs needed. It is part of your portion of the family investments on the last shipment. Consider returning to work with me and your brother this Season. There is more work than we can handle."

The direct look from his father left no argument, and for the first time in a long time, he felt the urge to accept and finally apologize.

"Come along, Robert," his mother said, breaking the spell.

His father patted his shoulder. "Do not overthink it, son."

Evan nodded. "Thank you."

Remaining at the doorway as the carriages ambled away, the envelope stuffed with money clutched in his hand brought more emotions than he was ready to deal with. It was obvious even without looking that his father had been overly generous. In the past, he would have not accepted it; he would have allowed pride to ensure his father he did not need it.

This time, however, he couldn't help but take it. He knew his father had invested heavily in several shipments on behalf of the family. However, since not working with them, he'd never been given a portion in the past.

It made sense, as he would have squandered it.

That his father had noticed he'd matured and could be trusted enough to receive the funds? All that happened since waking made him question the idea of seducing a woman to come up with money for the spice ship.

Perhaps, it was best to call off the entire deal.

He could return to work, tell the captain that he and his friends could not afford to sponsor the ship, and allow someone else to do it.

"Why are you standing in the doorway like a statue?" Grant asked. When Evan turned, his friend was walking back toward the dining room. "I must have more of the black pudding," he called out over his shoulder. "You?"

"I am full, but I will join you."

Upon sitting, he poured another cup of tea and studied Grant. "You left abruptly last night. I thought you planned to seek out your benefactor."

His friend's lips curved. "I did find someone who is willing to pay handsomely for my...company. She invited me for drinks tonight." Grant lifted a hefty serving of black pudding to his mouth. "Lady Gardenia Mackenzie has been itching to get her hands on me."

The thought of lying with a woman three times his age was enough to put Evan off from another portion of anything on the table.

"How is it you can be intimate with a woman so much older than you?" Evan asked. "I have never known you to be with anyone older than your mother."

Grant's eyes slid to the side as he considered his response. "It is easy to allow someone you are attracted to gain access to your heart. I do not wish to ever fall in love. I cannot allow it."

The statement made Evan study his friend. It was not the first time that Grant had alluded to not wishing to marry. However, this was the first time he made the statement that he did not wish to fall in love. In Evan's opinion, love was rare and only a lucky few could ever find it.

He doubted that it appeared unless one was somehow blessed in a manner that was hard to understand. There was attraction, sure, even deep caring. Love, that was something he often considered to be something made up by romantics who were influenced by poetry and novels.

"It will be comical if you develop deep feelings for someone old enough to be your grandmother," Evan said, and shuddered involuntarily.

Grant chuckled and shrugged. "Lady Gardenia has already insinuated that she wishes to gift me with something special. She has asked me what I wish for. I told her I'd think about it. What exactly is the amount we each should acquire?"

The woman in question was very wealthy. There were rumors that she hosted gatherings for those who preferred to be more sexually adventurous. However, since as yet none of his trio of friends had attended, Evan could not affirm the fact.

"I have a thought," Evan said. "Is she hosting only you or a group tomorrow night?"

"Why?" Grant asked between bites.

It took Evan a moment to come up with the correct way to get his point across. "If the rumors about the type of gatherings Lady Gardenia hosts are true, perhaps she wishes you to be part of the…entertainment."

Grant sat up straighter, his rounded eyes meeting Evan's. "Damn. I had not considered that. She did not specify."

Despite Evan finding humor in Grant's situation, he considered that it was imperative it only be Grant spending time with the woman in order for his friend to come up with the money.

"I would think if it were to be a group, she would have informed you."

His friend let out a breath. "I would think so as well."

"You have not told me why you left early," Evan asked again, wondering if it had something to do with Felicity.

"My sister became upset after dancing with you. Did you say anything to her that would be upsetting?"

Evan frowned while concentrating. "I do not believe we said one word."

"That is what she said. I believe my sister is ready to marry and is upset at the lack of a suitor. She and Hannah spoke about it last night and plan to discuss with Mother about hosting a gathering. I will also speak to Mother about this. She should host a dinner party to ensure a proper suitor is found for my sister."

Evan could not let the subject drop. "Is that what she stated? That she wishes to marry?"

"And have children," Grant replied. "Then the lovely Hannah decided she felt the same way. It was quite the ride home."

"The aroma drew me to enter without knocking," Henry announced, and made a beeline for the table. His eyes scanning over the offerings, he immediately lifted a plate. He began to pick and choose from the offerings.

Rosalie, who coddled Henry immediately, entered. "Allow me to warm whatever you wish to eat. I will bring hot tea as well."

While plopping food onto the plate, Henry looked to Grant. "What were you stating about Hannah?"

Grant blew out a breath. "I was commenting to Evan that both my sister and her friend have decided it is time to marry and have children."

At the last word, Henry began coughing, his face turning an alarming shade of red. Rosalie pounded his back, while Evan worried his friend was about to pass out from lack of air.

Finally, he managed to cough up the piece of bread and he scowled silently.

Evan let out a breath. "It must be a feminine inclination to think about children. The only time I consider it is when having a private interlude. I am careful with any assignations. I do not wish to father a child with someone I do not care for."

"I best get on with my task. I promised Felicity to speak to mother today." Grant stood and looked at Henry. "Anything to report? How many hopeful debutantes did you meet last night?"

"Too many to count. None that interested me." Henry blew out a breath. "It comes to mind that if I decide to marry, it would not be for months and I would be unable to collect a dowry in time for the sponsorship. Therefore, I may have to consider other means."

"You can always seduce someone's grandmother. That is what Grant is doing," Evan quipped, and could not keep from laughing at Grant's expression of annoyance.

Grant gave him a droll look. "It is only until I get the money."

"That may be a better recourse than attempting to get funding from a wily woman like Sorcha Robertson." Henry smiled at Rosalie, as she'd returned with hot tea and poured it into his cup.

What Henry said was true. It could be he was wasting his time. "I will give it another few days and then reevaluate my options. Perhaps we may have to consider that the entire plan is doomed."

Grant shrugged. "Interesting that you give up so soon. It is not like you, Evan."

"Does anyone know what Miles is up to?" Henry asked between bites.

Evan shook his head. "He explained to me that he can come up with his portion without participating in our plan. Ever the sportsman, he plans to come up with the needed money without delving into his own reserves."

Everyone grunted as they considered it. Grant spoke next. "I do think he will not have to try hard for it. People give more freely to those they know do not actually require it."

Leaving his friends in the dining room, Evan went upstairs to his bedchamber. He felt a need to bathe, but settled for washing up at the basin.

Once dressed in fresh clothes, he went to the window and considered what to do. Peering out, he noted it was a remarkably sunny day. The sunlight shone on the cobblestones below and sides of buildings.

Carts and carriages ambled by as people began their day. In truth, it felt awkward to not have a purpose day after day. He looked to the table where he'd placed the money his father had given him.

Actually, he did have a lot to do that day. First, he'd hire men to replace the entire roof then he'd consult his mother on whatever other items the house required. He wasn't about to order rugs and drapes, as he'd no idea where to start.

Then there was another matter to see to. He would visit Felicity and ensure all was well between them.

Any gentleman would call on a woman after a kiss like the one they'd shared.

At the thought, Sorcha came to mind. It was utterly disrespectful of him to be considering calling on someone else after spending the night.

"Ugh," he exclaimed. "What have I gotten myself into?"

"Sir?" Norman stood in the doorway. "Is something wrong?"

He whirled. "No. No. Just talking to myself. What is it, Norman?"

"You have a visitor. Miss Murray is here."

"Felicity?"

"Yes, sir."

He studied the man for a long moment. "Norman, call the men who patched the roof. Inform them I require them to replace the entire thing. Also, make an inventory of any household items that need to be replaced."

That Norman was not surprised at the requests meant he'd met with his father. He was probably the one who'd informed him of the amount needed for everything. Evan wondered if his father worried he'd not do the right thing.

Along with his butler, he went downstairs and found Felicity sitting in the parlor. Her hands folded in her lap, she presented a beautiful picture.

"Good morning." Evan walked closer, stopping at a chair and placing his hand on the back of it. "Is something wrong?"

Her green gaze met his and Evan's stomach dipped. That a woman had such an effect on a rogue like him was astounding in itself.

"No, nothing is wrong. I came to speak to my brother, but am informed he left with Henry."

"He did?" Evan turned toward the dining room, which was devoid of any evidence of the earlier meal. "They were just here."

She looked to the chair he stood behind and her brow furrowed. "Is something wrong with you? You seem to be hiding behind that chair."

Annoyed she noticed his hesitance, he rounded the chair and sat. "I was about to order tea."

Just then Rosalie entered with a tray that held a tea pot, cream, and two cups. She smiled at Evan and left.

Felicity busied herself pouring. "I wished to speak to my brother, so that, in turn, he'd speak to you about hosting an event here. It would be a perfect place to allow Hannah the opportunity to meet eligible men to marry."

"Here?"

She looked about the room, not seeming to notice the need for updates and repairs. "Why not?"

"I hear that you wish to find a suitor as well." Evan met her gaze, unable to help that his eyes wandered to her pouty pink lips. He cleared his throat. "We cannot host here. The house is about to go through renovations.

"Pity," Felicity said. "Can they not be put off for just a pair of weeks?"

In truth, it would take that long for anything to start. The last thing he wanted was for people to come there and see how far into disrepair the house had been allowed to fall.

"How about we consider early summer instead? By then the house will be more presentable. It will only be a pair of months."

Felicity sat back and sipped her tea, then lowering the cup, she let out a sigh. "Why did you kiss me like that last night?"

He'd wondered which of them would bring the subject up. More so, he'd hoped they would ignore it and pretend it never happened. Of course, knowing Felicity, she would ask.

"It felt right in that moment."

Lowering her gaze, she seemed to consider his reply. "It did feel right, I suppose. However, it was not the proper thing. Neither was you tossing me into the bushes."

"For that I do apologize. I did not wish to be found alone with you and give gossips fodder."

Her lovely eyes narrowed. "Or you did not wish for Sorcha to see us?"

The lass was very clever. It was best to be honest with her. "I prefer to kiss you than her."

"You are a rogue. And did you then, kiss her?"

Evan practically spit out the sip of tea he'd just taken.

"Grant plans to speak to your mother about hosting an event for you and Hannah. Perhaps he is at your house at the moment."

Giving him a knowing look, Felicity stood, so Evan did as well. They stood awkwardly, as if not sure what to do next. In his mind, he would hug her close, feeling once again the softness of her curves against him.

Felicity let out a sigh. "You and I should not be alone." It was practically a whisper. The words fell over him like a caress, and he almost closed his eyes.

"Why is that?" Evan took a step closer and peered down at the beauty whose chest lifted and lowered with each breath, mesmerizing him.

When she placed a hand on his forearm, heat scorched up to his chest. "Evan, I must go."

"Yes, of course."

Neither moved.

He leaned forward.

"Am I interrupting something?" Sorcha's tone left no question she knew exactly what would have happened if she'd not walked in.

Felicity turned to the woman. "You interrupted me telling Mister Macleod that he is a cad." With that, she swept from the room, leaving a trail of tantalizing scent.

CHAPTER SEVEN

S HE WALKED SO fast from the Macleod estate Ana could barely keep up. Once in the carriage, she finally let out a shaky breath. Whatever was she thinking, seeking out Evan? He was not the kind of man to marry, but instead, one who would forever be a rogue.

Thank God Sorcha Robertson arrived when she did. It proved that she'd been wrong in going to his house and hoping he'd declare himself.

She'd woven stupid fantasies in her head all night while reminiscing about the kiss they'd shared in the garden. Such an infatuated fool to have pushed aside the fact he'd discarded her into bushes straight after.

"Where to?" The coachman stared at her through the window.

Felicity fell back onto the seat and looked at Ana. "To the Kerrs', please."

"Is something wrong?" Ana asked. "You've gone pale."

It was no use trying to hide things; it had never been easy for Felicity to keep things secret. "I fooled myself into thinking Evan Macleod cared for me. Why do we romanticize things so?"

"Some men find it so very hard to accept being in love." Ana was married to the coachman. Both were in their thirties and very much in love. They lived in a small house on the edge of the Murray property with his mother, who cared for their three children. In Felicity's estimation, Ana had the perfect life.

"I must say that I envy you," Felicity admitted. "I wish for what you have."

Ana smiled widely. "I am blessed. Especially with a husband that allows me to work and get away from the wee ones for most of the day."

Upon arriving at Hannah's house, they found no one home. Disheartened that she could not commiserate with her closest friend, Felicity ordered the driver to take them home.

To her surprise, Grant was indeed at her house. In the parlor, he and her mother sat having tea with paper spread on the low table, from which adornments and the tea tray had been moved aside.

"What are you two plotting?" Felicity asked, removing her cloak and peering down at the lists her mother had penned.

"We are planning your debut into society," her mother replied, and jotted down a name, then scratched another off the list.

"I agree, Grant, Craig Gordon is much too old."

Felicity agreed, although the man in question was handsome. "Too old for what?"

"To marry you." Both her mother and brother replied at once.

"Oh." Felicity sat down. "It is ridiculous to plan a debut for me. I am much too old. My initial debut was ruined by the huge storms that year that lasted well into late spring. And then father fell ill. Horrible year."

"And that is why you deserve another." Her mother looked to Grant. "Oh yes, Calum Ross is a lovely young man."

"Calum Ross lives in Inverness," Felicity said.

"He's returned," Grant quipped. "Looks a bit haggard, but I am sure it is because of the bitter weather."

"Or he drinks too much," Felicity said, and frowned when her mother did not cross off his name.

"What if instead of a debut, it be more of a social event with a light suggestion of the reason. Do not outwardly state a debut, Mother. It would make me the laughingstock among our friends.

They will say I am desperate to marry. Which I am not, by the way. Actually, I may have changed my mind completely."

"Don't be silly, Felicity," her mother said, and then looked at Grant. "What about Richard Macleod?"

"No, absolutely not," Felicity exclaimed. "He is Evan's brother."

"What does that have to do with anything?" Grant asked.

There really was no answer that made sense.

His name stayed on the list.

Eventually, it was fun to watch Grant and her mother write down names as she found reasons for them to discard the person. In the end, they were left with a list of ten names, including Richard Macleod.

"This must be for Hannah as well," Felicity insisted. "She must marry and soon."

"What's the hurry?" Grant asked.

With the financial status of Hannah's family, it would be very hard to find a man who would marry her. However, there were plenty of men who cared little about the fact Hannah had no dowry.

"I am sure she will find someone to marry. She is a quite a beauty," her mother said. "Of course she will be included, and hopefully in a more intimate setting, find a suitor."

Despite the fact she had no plans to find a suitor herself, Felicity was excited at the prospect of entertaining at her house.

"You will be here, will you not, Grant?" She gave her brother a knowing look. "It will look badly if you are not."

"It is time for you and your father to speak and set things right. Whatever happened between you two needs to be put to rest." Their mother gave him a stern look. "I do not know why you insist on remaining away and spending your days as if with no family to call your own."

"It was Father who asked me to leave. I can't very well march back home and announce that I am living here."

"That is because of your roguish ways," Felicity said. "If you decide to become a proper gentleman and perhaps return to work with Father, then perhaps he will ask that you return home."

Grant blew out a breath. "I am perfectly well living with Evan."

"Two rogues who will end up old and smelly." Felicity stood and went to the doorway. "I will bring you soup and soft biscuits that you can chew."

Her mother let out a bark of laughter and shook her head. "Pay heed, Grant. Felicity may jest, but it could happen."

Grant looked to the ceiling. "Mother, if you do not require me for anything else, I have matters to see to."

"I will require you to see about ensuring the men on our list are indeed in good standing and not overwrought by debt or such."

"Yes, Mother," Grant replied, leaning down to kiss her cheek.

AS WAS HERS and Hannah's practice to volunteer weekly at a women's infirmary for the poor, Felicity entered the maternity wing and was immediately put to work by a nurse. "Quick, fetch bandages and bring them to me," the woman called out, pointing at a cabinet.

Behind a screen, a woman grunted in pain, her extended belly telling she was in the throes of labor.

"You should go back out behind the screen," the same nurse said. "You should not witness this."

Felicity ignored the woman and went closer. Taking the woman's hand, she smiled down at her. "How exciting that soon you will meet your wee one."

Despite the obvious distress, the woman managed a tight smile. "I can barely wait. Will ye please see about my husband? He is the one pacing outside the door, fraught with worry..." The woman stopped and groaned.

"Push when you're ready," the nurse instructed.

The woman did as she was told. Her entire body tightened with the exertion. When she stopped pushing, she looked back up at Felicity. "Tell him all is going well."

Felicity looked at the nurse, who nodded, and then turned her attention back to the woman. "One more push and the little one will be born."

As she rounded the divider, the woman let out a long moan. Moments later, a rowdy cry filled the room. Every woman there turned toward the sound.

The cries of a newborn had such an effect that soon everyone's face brightened at the sound of new life.

"Mister McKinney?" Felicity looked out from the entryway. There were several men who paced, worried expressions on their faces, but only one hurried toward her. "How is she? My wife? The child?"

Felicity could have kicked herself for not asking what the gender was. "The child is born. All is well. I will return with more information in a moment." She darted back inside, leaving the man with a happy and dazed expression.

Later that day, when she walked past the couple, now together, the husband's arms around his wife, both looking at the newborn with faces alight with love, Felicity faltered.

She'd not considered the closeness that came after a couple had a child. Creating a life together.

"Should we go?" Hannah approached, removing her apron. "I am going to accept your invitation for tea."

When her friend followed her line of sight and looked at the couple, she gave Felicity a knowing look. "Feeling the urgings, are you?"

"Urgings?"

Hannah nodded. "Mother says that there comes a time when a woman feels strong stirrings toward motherhood."

"I do not feel anything of the like," Felicity insisted, and turned to her friend. "Let's find a tea shop and rest for a bit."

Once settled at the small tea shop they preferred, Felicity leaned forward. "It has been a horrible time since the party at Sorcha Robertson's house."

"What do you mean?" Hannah asked.

"Well, the kiss. I told you about that. Followed by being tossed into the bushes. Most upsetting thing to ever happen."

It was obvious by Hannah's pretend cough that she fought not to laugh. "Evan is a cad."

"Something worse happened."

At this, Hannah's eyes widened. "What could possibly be worse than being kissed breathless and then tossed into bushes?"

"I romanticized the entire episode and went to his house."

"No."

"Yes. I went to his house. I think he was about to kiss me again. Then Sorcha appeared. She was all puffy and angry."

"She is a sea witch." Hannah blew out a breath. "Then again, perhaps it is good that there was an interruption. What if he did kiss you again? Are you in love with him?"

"Yes. Perhaps. No. Impossible."

The bell over the door rang, and both looked to see Miles Johnstone enter. The lord was ravishing in a rich burgundy day jacket and riding boots. He didn't see them and walked straight to the counter.

"He would be a wonderful match for you," Hannah said as she studied the lord's profile. "I bet he is a romantic."

Felicity frowned in the direction of Miles. "I do not have the pedigree. I bet he will marry someone from London or local high society."

Seeming to sense their regard, Miles turned to them after completing his purchase. He neared the table and nodded in greeting. "Ladies."

"Lord Johnstone," Felicity began. "I would think your household would send someone for such trivial purchases."

His lips curved into a smile, showcasing straight white teeth. "I am on my way to visit my parents. Thought to stop and purchase Mother's favorite tea."

"Very kind of you, my lord," Hannah said with a slight blush. It was obvious she was not unaffected by his handsome presence.

For a moment, the lord studied her friend; it was as if he'd not noticed her before. "I do not like to show up anywhere empty handed. Besides, Mother and I will share it."

With another nod, he bid them farewell and walked out.

"You like him," Felicity said, a wide smile spreading across her face. "You are enamored with Miles Johnstone."

Hannah rolled her eyes. "Honestly, who isn't? The man is absolutely beautiful." Her right shoulder lifted and lowered. "It is not as if he'd ever notice me. Besides, with my family's standing, I could never aspire to a man like him."

"Hmm, I wonder." Felicity slid a look to the door. "I wonder who we can match you with."

FEELING RESTLESS, FELICITY walked through the garden just outside the family parlor. Her mind remained on the conversation with Hannah. Her friend had suggested that it could be possible she'd fallen in love with Evan.

Love? If that was true, she had to do something immediately to stop her emotions. The last thing she needed was to feel enamored with a rogue like Evan Macleod.

A cat hopped atop the wall that ran along the east side of the property. The rascal belonged to a couple who lived nearby. The black and white cat visited often, possibly because Ana fed it.

Its yellow eyes glanced at her, then finding her inadequate, the feline jumped gracefully and rushed to the kitchen door.

Felicity followed its progress and then settled back in a chair and let out a sigh as the sun warmed her skin.

A picture of Evan's face formed, and she allowed her eyelids to fall. The way his arms had felt around her was something she'd never forget. The press of his lips over hers, the way he'd pulled her against him.

"Oh my," Felicity said. Her eyes flew open and she fanned her face. The sun was a bit too warm.

CHAPTER EIGHT

"**I** DO NOT believe her," Sorcha repeated, lifting a brow. "Why was Felicity Murray really here?"

The morning had turned to afternoon and still the woman insisted on rehashing the same conversation. In truth, Evan did not care what she thought. However, heeding his brother's advice, he tried to tread carefully.

"Her brother lives here. She came seeking him out."

"Why would she call you a cad then?"

Of course he wished to tell her the truth about the kiss and perhaps it would send her away. However, he wasn't about to say something that could bring some sort of retribution on Felicity.

"Felicity, Grant, and I have been friends since childhood, and we are always at odds over one thing or another. I am sure it has something to do with the fact that Grant and I have failed to do something. It is never a serious matter with Felicity."

To his astonishment, Sorcha seemed to believe him. "I did not come here to speak about the lass. Instead, I wanted to speak to you about the trip. I am to meet with several others who plan to go. I will purchase passage for two."

"There is a venture that other business partners and I are about to embark on. I am working tirelessly to come up with my portion of the capital. It is impossible for me to travel at the moment. I have business to see to."

Sorcha shrugged. "What is the amount you need? I would not mind being part of this venture if it will be turning a profit."

"The people involved are the only ones contributing, I'm afraid." He was on the brink of acquiring the money. He was sure the amount would not be a hardship for Sorcha.

The woman studied him for a long moment. "I can gift you the money. Then you will be free to travel with me."

Evan let out a breath. "That you enjoy my company so much is flattering." He wasn't sure how to proceed. On one hand, this was the plan. To use roguish charm to get the money to sponsor the ship. However, something did not sit right with him. This was surely the most inopportune time to grow a conscience.

"I cannot accept your generous offer."

His stomach sunk and chest constricted to the point he wondered if he was having a heart attack. He must have turned pale because Sorcha's eyes widened.

"Are you unwell?"

After several deep breaths, he regained composure. "I am. I just realized I am dreadfully late to meet with my father. Can I escort you somewhere?"

"I hope this is a way to come up with the money so you can accompany me." Sorcha lifted on her toes and placed a kiss to his lips. "My carriage awaits. Come to see me tomorrow night."

Evan waited until the door closed and then another several beats before he grunted out loud. "What have I done? What is wrong with me?"

"Sir?" Norman asked, looking about the room. "Is someone here?"

"No, no one." Evan lowered to a chair. "What is it, Norman?"

"The roof repair is to begin tomorrow morning."

"Very good. Can you have my horse brought around? I have errands to see about."

HIS FIRST STOP was to his family home. His mother was ecstatic at the idea of shopping for anything needed for the house.

"You must come along to help. It would be lovely to get your perspective."

He gave his mother a droll look. "What if you ask Felicity Murray to go with you? She's told Grant she hopes to marry soon. She would probably welcome the experience."

"That is a grand idea," his mother exclaimed, giving him a curious look. "Is she special to you?"

His stomach tumbled at the question and he did his best to ignore it. "We have known each other since childhood; of course she matters to me." Deciding it was best to leave before he spilled all his emotions, Evan stood. "I best go. I have an appointment I cannot be late for." Evan hurried to the door to avoid any more questions from his mother.

MACLEOD IMPORTS STOOD proudly on the corner of Ingram and George Street. The two-story structure had been built by his grandfather, the founder of the thriving business. Over time, his father had opted to remain in the same building, although it had been expanded quite a bit.

The front area was vast, shelves along one entire side of the space filled to capacity with different types of textiles, linens, cookery, wool, and other items from which shops could purchase for their own inventory.

In the center of the area were crates, some open, others recently prepared and about to be sent out for delivery.

The city had grown, and with it, consumerism. New grocers, confectioners, bakers, tobacconists, perfumers, wigmakers, hairdressers, haberdashers, drapers, hatters, glovers, breeches-makers, and stay-makers seemed to be constantly opening. It all meant that suppliers like his father fought to keep up with the demand.

Evan took in the large space, realizing his father had been right to hold on to their business through the hard years after his grandfather's death. How he and Richard managed everything made him proud and sad at the same time. He'd not been there to help, to do his part, all because of pride.

At hearing voices and applause, he walked to a secondary and smaller area. Here there were several desks piled with invoices. No one sat at the desks; instead, everyone stood and was facing the front of the room where his brother and father stood.

"Congratulations, Anthony, you've earned this promotion," his father said to a man who stood next to him, and once again, everyone clapped.

After the newly promoted man went back to the group, face beaming as several clapped him on the back, his father made a few announcements about hours and expectations. The entire time Richard stood near with an expression of pride as he concentrated on what their father said.

When his father saw Evan standing at the back of the room, he hesitated just enough that Richard noticed his presence. The workers were dispersing at that moment, so no one else seemed to take notice. Several who walked past Evan toward the front room gave him a curious look but did not say anything.

He wondered what was said about him to the workers, about why he was not part of the company.

"I wasn't aware you woke this early," Richard said, walking past and on to the front area where a team of men seemed to be awaiting directions.

His brother handed out papers, directing which items would be delivered that day and where. After, he turned to a pair of women, who peppered him with question after question. The entire time, Richard remained calm, and despite Evan noting that some of the questions were redundant, he answered each one and then gave them directions as to what had to be done first.

Deciding to seek out his father, Evan went to where the workers had gathered, and like Richard, his father spoke to a group of men, giving them a list of priorities for the day.

Just then a pair of men rushed in stating they had to unload items and the back entry was blocked.

His father motioned to Anthony. "I trust you can take care of the issue."

When he turned to Evan, his father grinned. "Twice in one week. I am surprised to see you." Robert Macleod walked toward his office, motioning for Evan to follow.

Once inside, he invited Evan to sit. "Tea?"

"Yes, thank you." Evan watched as his father went to the door and gestured to one of the women who'd been talking to Richard. "Tea for two please, Catriona."

His father turned his attention back to Evan. "If this is about the money, you do not have to report to me what you are doing with it. I trust you to do what is necessary. If you require more, let me know."

"It is not about the money, although it is much needed. Repairs on the roof start soon and Mother is helping with replacements that are needed."

His father chuckled. "I am sure she is thrilled at the idea."

"Father," Evan started, his throat suddenly dry. He wondered how long before the tea came. Thankfully, Catriona, hurried in, placed a tray between them, and hurried back out.

"It is a busy time as of late, barely any opportunity to take a break." The smile on his father's face told he did not mind it one bit.

"I came to apologize. I have been a horrible son to not have come sooner and taken responsibility for all my shortcomings. My entire inheritance is gone except for a small investment that has been paying just enough." Evan blinked away the moisture in his eyes and he was grateful for the cup of tea his father handed him.

His father's gaze was warm. "We are all young and foolish at least once in our lives."

"Richard never was," Evan mused.

"He had his moments," his father replied with a chuckle. "I must admit to hoping you'd come around sooner than this. Pride is not a good counselor, son."

Evan nodded. "I am in total agreement, Father."

"What do you plan to do now?" His father studied him. "Do you plan to continue this life of leisure you have been pursuing?"

"No. Which is what I need to speak to you about."

His father remained quiet, giving him time to put his words in order and swallow past the dryness of his throat.

"First of all, I want to let you know that I have not been able to come up with enough money as yet to sponsor the ship; however, along with Miles, Grant, and Henry, we are determined and working on it."

"I see." His father nodded. "I gave my friend my word that you would sponsor it. You have two months yet before he has to leave. There are plenty of people who will be willing to sponsor it, your brother and I included. However, I have faith you will do it."

"I will…we will."

"What else, son? I'm afraid I have much to do."

"Is there a position here that I could fill?" Evan blurted. "I do not mind menial work to start. I know there is much I have to learn about how things work…here." Despite preparing for what he'd say, his entire body became rigid, his shoulders and jaw tight. It would not be surprising if his father took this opportunity to teach him a lesson.

"Your position was never filled, Evan. Your office is like you left it twelve years ago when you walked away."

"What?" Evan stood and went to the closed door that was on the left side of his father's. Richard's office was on the right. He opened the door, and true to what his father had said, his office was exactly as he'd left it.

"It will take a while for you to catch up with the processes. You can shadow me, but don't expect me to be easy on you," Richard said from behind him.

Evan was too overcome with emotion to do more than nod. Thankfully, his brother must have realized it because he walked to their father's office, giving him a moment to compose himself.

"I have just received an invitation to a gathering at the Murrays' house. Rather odd, do you not think?" Evan heard Richard say.

"Why would it be odd? They are family friends; you and your brother have known each other since childhood," their father said.

Richard let out a breath. "This is obviously the kind of gathering for when a young woman seeks suitors."

At the words, Evan walked over to his brother and took the invitation from his hand. It was worded in a way that made it obvious it was to be a dinner party for singles only. He wondered if he was invited.

This was the event that Grant had spoken about.

"You look about to burst," Richard quipped. "I'm sure yours is being delivered as we speak."

CHAPTER NINE

FELICITY WAS SHOCKED when Evan's mother invited her shopping. At the same time, she jumped at the opportunity. It was a chance to get out of the house and all the preparations for the dinner party that she wished never to have asked for. The more she considered that she'd either be humiliated because no one would court her or mortified when someone she did not care for did, the more she regretted the idea.

"Richard was surprised to be invited to the dinner party on Friday," Mrs. Macleod announced while they waited for the samples of drapery and upholstery fabric to be packaged, along with a pair of pillows.

"I am not sure who Mother has invited. I should check the list. I hope he will accept the invitation." Felicity tried to remember if she'd seen Richard lately. She'd always thought of him as aloof, and spent more time with his nose in books or following his father to work than with Grant and Evan when they were younger. He was attractive, from what she remembered. "I do not believe to have seen him since returning."

"Probably not. He rarely goes anywhere other than the gentlemen's club or to work. He takes after his father."

"Where to next?" Felicity asked with a grin. She was actually enjoying the task of decorating Evan's home and had taken extra care when choosing fabrics that coordinated nicely.

"Let's stop for tea. After, we will go to the house to inspect and ensure Evan gave me the complete list."

The tea shop was bustling with activity; thankfully, a couple got up just as they entered, so a table was free. Once tea was ordered, Felicity studied those in the shop. There were mostly women of all ages, mothers with daughters and groups of friends. "Mrs. Macleod, do you wish to have had a daughter?"

"All the time," the woman replied in a wistful tone. "That is why I am so enjoying your company. I cannot wait for my sons to marry so I can have daughters-in-law. Hopefully, I will not be one of those overbearing monsters."

At the words, Felicity laughed. "I assure you, whoever your daughters-in-law are, they will treasure you."

Tea was served along with a scone each and lemon curd. At another table, a bright color caught Felicity's gaze. It was hard not to roll her eyes at seeing Sorcha Robertson and two companions. The women, in their thirties, wore too much rouge for the time of day.

Sorcha caught sight of them and practically jumped to her feet. As the woman neared, Felicity pretended not to notice her.

"Mrs. Macleod, I thought that was you," Sorcha exclaimed as if she just happened to be walking past. "It is so nice to see you," she purred.

Her companion looked up at the woman and smiled. "Good afternoon, Sorcha. You look as if headed for a social event."

When Sorcha's brow pinched, Felicity waited for her reply. "Yes, well, I am here meeting friends for tea. Did Evan tell you I have invited him on an extended holiday?"

At the question, Mrs. Macleod coughed and gasped, attempting to catch her breath. Felicity scowled at Sorcha. "You should return to your friends. This is not the place for such an announcement."

The woman seemed to realize her mistake and her eyes widened. "I do apologize." She backed up and hurried away.

"Come, we must go to Evan's house immediately." Mrs. Macleod stood, leaving the tea and food, and walked toward the door.

Felicity had to run to keep up with Mrs. Macleod. The carriage driver gave her a questioning look when a red-faced Mrs. Macleod barked out orders to hurry to Evan's house.

It was a short trip. A horse was tethered outside, and Felicity recognized it as Evan's. It seemed he was either about to leave or had just arrived.

Once again, she hurried to keep up with a very angry Mrs. Macleod, who'd barely spoken in the carriage.

"Evan, I must speak to you immediately," she called out from the entryway.

Grant rushed out from the parlor. "What happened?"

Mrs. Macleod turned to him. "Where is my son?"

"Upstairs," Grant replied, pointing to the stairs, and then rushed up taking two at a time. "I will fetch him."

"I best go find a place to sit," Felicity offered.

"You will do no such thing. You are my witness to what the awful harpy just said." The statement did not leave any room for argument, so Felicity remained rooted to the spot.

Moments later, Evan hurried down the stairs. He was without a cravat or coat. It seemed he was in the middle of changing.

"I apologize, Mother. I spilled ink all over myself and—"

"I do not care about any of that. Why would that horrible woman inform me that you and she are to go on extended holiday? Evan, you best measure your reply."

Felicity had never seen Evan's mother so angry. She was compelled to take a step sideways to avoid being drawn into the conversation.

"I do not know what you are referring to, Mother. I am not to go on holiday. I have only just started to—"

"Sorcha Robertson," Mrs. Macleod bit out, jaw clenched, "felt compelled to interrupt us at tea to inform me of your plans to travel on holiday."

"Oh." Evan looked to Felicity.

Angry herself that he was to go with that woman, she frowned at him. "She said it in public, where others could overhear."

At her statement, Evan's expression turned to stone. "I assure you, Mother. I have not made any plans whatsoever to go on holiday with her."

"It best be true. She ruined what was a lovely day."

"Continue your day; do not allow her to cloud over it. I will send a message and ensure she does not repeat this type of action. Or believes that we are to go anywhere together."

Mrs. Macleod glared up at her son. "I do not care for your roguish reputation in the least. I would however hope that your...interactions are with someone more...discreet."

At his mother's words, Evan inhaled sharply. "Understood."

"Come, Felicity, I require to sit and calm before we continue with our project. The appeal of it lost its luster at considering who my son will entertain in this house."

"Mother, a word," Evan said as they walked away. Felicity kept going, not wishing to be an interloper any longer. In truth, at Mrs. Macleod's words, she too lost her excitement.

When Felicity entered the parlor, Grant gave her a bewildered look. "Sounds as if she is rather upset."

"Of course she is. Both she and our mother tire of all the rumors of you and Evan's roguish behavior. There comes a point when they will no longer tolerate it. I believe Mrs. Macleod has reached her limit."

"Is that understood?" Mrs. Macleod's voice carried to them. "It must stop. I should not have to pay for your actions. You must comport yourself like a gentleman from this point forward. I will not tolerate being embarrassed like today ever again."

Whatever Evan replied was too soft for Felicity to overhear, but she figured he had been roundly chastised by his mother. It was hard not to peek out the doorway to see his expression.

Moments later, Mrs. Macleod entered and sat. She slid a look to Grant. "I will be speaking to your mother as well. All of this nonsense must stop."

Grant's eyes rounded. "Yes, ma'am."

"Now," Mrs. Macleod said, looking about the room. "What do you think of this room?" She glanced to Grant. "Be a dear and retrieve our purchases from the carriage."

Grant almost ran from the room.

Felicity giggled. "They both needed a good chastisement. I hope Mother sees to Grant."

Mrs. Macleod shook her head. "It was a long time coming."

THE DRESSMAKER FINALLY put her tape measure down and nodded at Felicity. "That will do for now. I will be there day after tomorrow for final fittings."

She stepped down from the small, elevated platform. Her mother smiled at the dressmaker and pulled out a bolt of dark blue fabric. The color was rich and deep. "I am thinking this would be a beautiful color for the end of Season ball. She would stand out among all the pastels."

The dressmaker grinned. "I picked it out thinking of a brunette. I agree, it will most definitely stand out."

"It is beautiful," Felicity said, reaching out to touch the soft fabric.

"We must have the dress ready no later than Thursday morning," her mother reminded the dressmaker while Felicity changed back into her afternoon gown.

They walked out of the shop and into the carriage.

"We have five gentlemen who I am sure will be suitors for you and three who I think will appreciate Hannah." Her mother sighed and looked out at the passing scenery. "This is a time you should do your best to enjoy. Such a special time in your life."

"Who are the five?" Felicity asked, genuinely curious.

"That I can remember so far Henry Campbell, Lachlan Sutherland, Scott Douglas and oh, I don't remember... Oh yes, Richard Macleod has accepted."

"Richard Macleod? How odd," Felicity replied. "I didn't think he ever socialized."

"He is rather elusive and stoic young man, but your father likes him."

Felicity blew out a breath. "Please do not use how Father feels about a person as a measurement tool."

Her mother laughed. "I promise not to."

As they rode toward home, she got up the courage to ask about Evan. "Am I to assume that since you invited Richard, you did not invite Evan?"

"Oh he was invited. Grant insisted."

"And?"

"He has not replied." Her mother studied her. "Your father would not approve of Evan. He has no ambitions, and with a reputation like his, I am not sure if he will ever change."

"In truth, Mother, with each passing day, I am beginning to consider that I prefer not to marry at all."

Her mother gave her a knowing look. "Unless it is Evan Macleod."

At first, she started to deny it, but then she decided it was best to sit back and consider why everyone seemed to be aware of how she felt.

"By the way," her mother started. "Whatever you did with the painting, retrieve it and get rid of the monstrosity in the parlor before Friday."

Felicity had totally forgotten about that incident. "Hopefully the shopkeeper has not sold ours yet."

She called out to the driver to take them to the antiquities shop where she'd sold the painting. The owner was glad to exchange it for the "right" one, as the one he'd acquired had yet to sell. He agreed to send someone to the house that very afternoon.

Feeling a bit guilty, Felicity returned to the carriage, the driver behind her with the painting. "He will send someone to fetch the other painting this afternoon."

"Good." Her mother gave her a warning look. "Ensure you are present to oversee the exchange. I am going to visit Lilian Macleod. She invited me for afternoon tea."

"Oh goodness," Felicity said, knowing the woman would probably bring up what happened with Evan. It would not do in the least if she did. "Must you go? There is still so much to get done before Friday."

"All is in order," her mother replied. "Besides, I enjoy Lilian's company."

It was a bit later that Felicity looked up from writing a letter in the sitting room after her butler cleared his throat.

"Someone is here for you, Miss," Gerard announced.

"Finally." Felicity went to the hallway where the ugly painting had been wrapped and was ready to be taken. She stopped when noting it was Evan who entered, her mouth forming an *O*.

"Felicity," he said in way of greeting.

Unsure of what to do, she looked past him to the butler. "When the man arrives from the antiquities shop, ensure he takes that painting." She pointed at the wall and then motioned for Evan to follow her to the sitting room.

He looked handsome as always, this time dressed casually wearing a white shirt left open at the throat and light tan trousers. His jacket was a light grey fabric, and he wore low boots.

"I came to apologize for yesterday."

She motioned for him to sit. "Whatever for?"

"What you were witness to at the tea shop and later with my mother." He gave her a look she could only describe as discomfited.

"Ha," Felicity exclaimed. "It must have been mortifying for you. I agreed with every word your mother stated. The nerve of that woman approaching her in public like that. I hope you will speak to her about her actions."

"What happened is the reason why I must turn down the invitation to your dinner party." He gave her a pained look. "I hope you understand."

She did. However, her heart did not seem to. It was as if someone reached into her chest and squeezed it.

"You'd considered coming?"

"Yes, I had. The day you came to the house, I hurried from the textile warehouse to see if I'd received an invite."

At a loss, she studied him. "I do not understand. Had you planned to..." She swallowed. "To pursue a relationship with me?"

"I had...yes."

She stood and went to the open French doors. Evan followed. The fresh air helped her breathe. "I am not sure what to think."

He rubbed his palms down his thighs and looked past her, seeming suddenly nervous. "Felicity, you occupy my every waking moment. You are the perfect combination of beauty and feist. There is nothing I do not admire about you. That every man doesn't fall at your feet makes me wonder why. I am fortunate to know you."

"Evan," she replied, unable to believe what he'd just uttered. Her heart galloped so fast and so hard she was sure he could hear it.

"It doesn't matter now, does it?" he said in a tight voice. "I am sure the gossips have already spread what happened."

Turning, she found herself practically against him. "I doubt it was overheard by more than one table."

"It may be enough. Mother is right; my actions are leading things in an ugly direction. It is probably best I leave Glasgow for a while and allow things to simmer down. My father requires someone to go and proffer items for the business. He is asking for volunteers to travel to Portugal."

He seemed startled when she placed her hand on his forearm. "Don't go, Evan. It is not as bad as it seems."

When he looked at her, she was lost in his dark eyes. "How could I ever deny you anything?" The corners of his lips lifted. "I am besotted with you, Felicity. I can no longer deny it."

Her breath caught. It could not be true. "Do not toy with

me." She was about to take a step away when his arms circled her, and his mouth took hers.

Felicity clung to him as they continued to kiss; all thought was gone other than falling under the spell of his mouth and the feel of his hard body against hers.

When they broke the kiss, both breathed heavily. "I should go."

"We should speak first, Evan. You cannot leave without us coming to some sort of agreement. The dinner...it will take place the day after tomorrow."

An expression of pain crossed his features. "It would be best if you choose another as a suitor."

Patience had never been one of her virtues, and Felicity was short on it today. "Your brother, for instance?"

"You wouldn't dare." By his expression, he very much believed she would.

"Of course I would."

He rested his forehead against hers and closed his eyes. "If you truly feel strongly for me, please wait. We have to wait for this all to blow over; otherwise, your parents will never allow you to be with me."

A gentle sensation fell over her and Felicity knew that no one would make her as happy as Evan. Despite his reputation and a myriad of past transgressions, her heart was forever his.

"You are who I constantly think about as well," Felicity began and smiled up at him. "Evan, I cannot fathom anyone else but you. You see, I feel as if without you, I am not tethered, not fully formed. It is as if you and only you finish me." At his incredulous expression, she smiled. "Of course we must wait. I have to be sure you will not return to being a rogue. I will not marry you if you dare step past another woman's threshold for any reason whatsoever. Your mother excluded, of course."

His lips twitched with a hint of a smile. "I accept your challenge and will be as chaste as a virgin until you and I..." He paused and took a deep breath. "Marry."

At his last word, Felicity stared at him, her mouth falling open. "I cannot believe you said the words. That you wish for us to marry." A giggle escaped.

"That is my intention, yes. But I will not ask you properly until a few weeks pass. First we must wait."

As much as she wanted to throw caution to the wind, to say to hell with all the restrictions and conventions of society, Felicity knew it had to be as Evan said. They had to wait, and first she had to figure out how to get through Friday.

"You must come on Friday. My parents must see that you are interested. It is imperative that you not seem the indifferent scoundrel they believe you to be."

"Scoundrel?" His right eyebrow hitched. "Hmmm."

Felicity giggled. "I made that up. I think they just consider you a rogue, a consummate ladies' man."

"I have been careless about my reputation. Not caring much what people think. However, I am making strides to correct the mistakes of my past. I have begun working at my family business. I will come on Friday."

"You have?" Felicity took his hand and pulled him to sit at a settee made for two. "Tell me about it?"

There was commotion in the hallway; Gerard peered in and shook his head. "They took the wrong item again."

"What do you mean?" Felicity rushed to the doorway. "I thought you were to oversee it." She glared at the ugly painting resting against the wall.

Gerard blew out a breath. "I was indisposed when he arrived. Ana saw to it and must have thought the wrapped one was a new purchase and gave the man the one on the wall there."

"Oh no." Felicity turned to Evan. "I require your help. We must stop him before he arrives at the shop."

Evan lifted the portrait and they rushed out to his carriage. "To the antiquities shop," he instructed the driver. "Hurry."

Thankfully, they caught up with the man rather quickly, as he'd stopped to purchase street food.

"Aye, what are you doing?" He hurried toward them when Evan yanked the portrait from the back of the cart and then lifted the wrapped one.

"You took the wrong one," Felicity called out from the carriage. "I do apologize for surprising you."

The man stood with his meal in hand, staring at them. "It's all right, I suppose." He grinned when Evan gave him a coin.

"For your troubles."

When Evan returned to the carriage, he shook his head. "Will life ever be boring with you?"

"Perhaps not, but now we must return to my house immediately. I cannot be seen alone with you."

He sat next to her and pulled her to his side. "Very well." Pressing a kiss to her temple, he let out a breath. "Waiting will be quite hard."

"You must deal with that Sorcha creature. Ensure she is aware that you will not be seeing her again."

"I will take care of it first thing."

When they arrived back at Felicity's house, there was another carriage in front. They slowed across the street and watched as Hannah and her mother walked to the front door.

"Oh dear," Felicity exclaimed. "I have to hurry."

With a fast kiss to his surprised lips, she threw the carriage door open and hurried out.

She raced across the street to the walkway of her own front door. Both Hannah and her mother looked at her and then across to where Evan's carriage remained.

"Decided to go for a short walk. Lost track of time."

"Is that so?" Hannah's mother asked, and looked across the street.

Evan crossed the street carrying the portrait she'd gone to reclaim. "Thank you for allowing me to try this at my house," he said in an attempt to seem as if he'd just arrived.

Both Hannah and her mother gave Felicity incredulous looks. Mrs. Kerr's was the disapproving kind.

"You are so welcome," Felicity said, keeping up the pretense. "Let us all go inside."

Once inside, he hung up the painting with care as they looked on, instructing him to slide it up and down until it was straight.

"Will you remain for tea?" Hannah asked Evan, who shook his head.

"I cannot, there is something I must see about." He gave Felicity a reassuring look. "Enjoy your afternoon, ladies."

Mrs. Kerr watched him until the door closed, lips pressed together. Thankfully, she did not comment.

They adjourned to the sitting room, and moments later, her mother entered, followed by a maid who carried flowers and other items that she'd purchased.

The entire time, Felicity held her breath, hoping Mrs. Kerr would not mention that Evan had been there.

CHAPTER TEN

E VAN PACED IN front of Sorcha's house. He'd promised Felicity not to cross a woman's threshold, which made the current situation awkward.

The butler had gone to fetch Sorcha, returned with a message for Evan to come inside, and he'd then sent back a reply that he could not.

It was but a short moment later that an irate Sorcha walked out and motioned to a side garden where they could have a bit more privacy.

"Why are you refusing to come inside, darling? Is something wrong?"

Was the woman so self-absorbed that she'd not considered how upset his mother had been at her outburst at the tea shop?

"It is best that I be frank. You crossed the line when speaking to my mother yesterday. How dare you speak with such liberty after only a tryst between us?"

"A tryst?" Sorcha was incredulous. "Is that all it was to you? We plan to travel—"

"I never accepted. I was clear in stating that I had matters to see to about here."

"And I offered to help with what you had to do so you could come. You did not say that you were not coming with me. All I did was inform your mother that we were to travel."

Evan knew he had to end things in a way that would not bring her ire; however, he doubted it would be easy. "Sorcha, I cannot continue to see you. It was but one night. An enjoyable one, but at this time, it is best for me to step away."

"I see." An icy demeanor fell over her, and when she lifted her gaze, it was with menacing calculation. "Is this about that Murray twit? You must realize she will never satisfy you. You will be crossing my doorstep again after but a few weeks."

"This is about your lack of respect toward my mother. I will never tolerate anyone distressing her in public the way you did. It is inexcusable, and I will not allow it."

Sorcha let out a most unladylike snort. "I find it childish for you to be so offended over something as trivial as me mentioning a trip."

"My mother was overly distressed at your announcement. What do you think those nearby thought about an unmarried man and woman traveling together?"

"The only one who overheard was Felicity Murray. She probably influenced your mother—"

"Enough!" Evan stood to his full height. "Goodbye, Sorcha. Do not speak to me again."

"Evan," Sorcha called out. "You will be sorry for this."

As he got into the carriage and headed toward the shop, he wondered if indeed he would be sorrier than he already was for becoming entangled with her.

"WHAT IS EVERYONE'S progress?" Henry asked the following evening at Evan's house. As agreed, they'd come together to discuss the sponsorship.

Miles stretched his long legs and crossed them at the ankles. "I have an idea of how to acquire my portion. I have been distracted with a family issue, but will be able to concentrate on the project after this week." He lifted the glass of brandy to his lips.

"It is harder than I expected," Henry said. "Although I have won several games, it is slow going to gather the amount needed. I've decided against marrying a young debutante. They are all so innocent and so anxious." He blew out a breath. "Although, if I cannot come up with my portion, I may change my mind again. We will see."

"What about you?" Grant asked Evan. "Now that you have returned to the work force, you have less time for other pursuits."

Evan drank down the contents of his glass and then told everyone what Sorcha had done and how upset his mother had been.

"As you can guess, that means I have to restart my plan. I do have about a quarter of it. I have decided against acquiring the rest from a woman and must see if there is a way to get an advance on my salary for the rest. Once the ship returns, I can repay it without a problem."

"What if it sinks?" Grant asked with a smirk. "Or pirates attack?"

"Then I will work for years without salary," Evan said. "It will not bother me. I owe my father as much."

"What about you, Grant?" Evan asked.

His friend smiled widely. "I will have it soon."

"Looks as if we all have a plan, and only one of us has the money required," Henry stated. He looked at Miles. "Of course, you had it before we started. Hopefully, for our sake, to keep things on a level playing field, you will acquire the capital by other means."

Miles laughed. "I will not use my own money. I have a plan in place. Once I am free, I assure you to begin the process. By the way, Grant, who all is going to your sister's event tomorrow night?"

At the question, Evan sat straighter, his attention on Grant.

His friend shrugged. "Frankly, I cannot wait for the evening to come and go. Despite a few acceptable candidates..." he looked around the room, "present company included, I am certain my sister will pick someone on her own that may or not attend."

"I suspect the same," Evan said. "But it will be interesting to see who tries to force his way into her heart." He eyed the others in the room. "Let me warn each of you that I do intend to court Felicity Murray."

"What?" Grant sat up and gawked. "You?"

Evan prepared to be charged and thrown to the ground. "Yes, after speaking with your sister yesterday afternoon, we decided that we have grown fond of each other."

As expected, Grant stood and neared. His friend towered over him as Evan remained seated. "You are aware I care for you as a brother. However, I know all you have done as of late. I do not approve of you courting my sister. You are sleeping with Sorcha Robertson...for one."

"I ended all ties with her upon leaving Felicity's company."

"And what of..." Grant seemed to struggle to keep from hitting him. Finally, he blew out a harsh breath. "No."

Miles and Henry exchanged looks, both entranced by the scene before them.

"What do you mean no?" Evan said. "You and I are friends. I would not oppose you marrying—"

"Your brother?" Grant interrupted. "You do not have a sister, so you cannot possibly understand."

"I care for Felicity and will do my best to be a good husband to her."

When Grant took a breath, Henry jumped to his feet. "Do not say something you will regret. We all know each other well enough. You must admit never to have heard Evan state wishing to be husband to anyone. I for one believe him to be in love."

"Love," Miles added, "is unpredictable, unexpected, and without prejudice for who the other person is." His handsome face was stern. "I believe you, Evan—that you are indeed in love with Miss Felicity. At the same time, I understand you, Grant." He waved around the room. "I would worry if any of you professed to be in love with my sister."

At the statement, every eye locked onto Miles.

It was Henry who found his voice. "Have I met your sister?"

Miles shook his head. "She has not debuted as of yet. Her name is Penelope, and she is beautiful, delicate, and absolutely off limits."

It was a long moment that everyone eyed Miles, no doubt attempting to picture his face in a more feminine way. None found it appealing by the way they decided not to pursue the line of questioning.

"So it seems that brothers are protective sorts," Evan said, pushing to his feet and facing Grant. "Very well, so you do not approve. Yet you will not have a problem with my boring brother, or any of the sops on the list you and your mother made?"

"It is that I wish my sister to be happy and to have a faithful husband. I understand why you are working now and making strides toward setting yourself up to be a good match. I appreciate it. My answer remains no." Grant sneered at him and went to the sidebar to refill his glass.

Despite his efforts, Evan could not blame his friend. Even with a family of means, Evan would never be wealthy unless the ship investment was made and it paid off. There were always unexpected things that could happen at sea. The investment was not without its risks. Like a sodden cloak, a weight came over him. Who did he think he was to deserve Felicity? Despite having recently made strides toward a better way of living, he was still without proper means to offer a wife. That she considered him worthy was a miracle. As it stood, he would only be a detriment to her life.

Grant started to say something, but Evan stopped him. "Perhaps you are right. That I should not have pursued your sister. If you'll excuse me, gentlemen. I have an early morning." He went up the stairs, knowing his friends were exchanging questioning looks at his lack of attempting to convince Grant more.

THE HOUSE WAS bright, candlelit with candelabras on every possible surface. A string quartet had set up in the parlor, the music wafting throughout the house. In the sitting room, her mother and Mrs. Kerr kept company with a pair of older women who were there to help keep an eye on the younger women and gentlemen who would be arriving soon.

Felicity walked down the hallway to where the dining room had been set. She glanced about the room with its long table down the center that was resplendent with beautiful flowers, the china and silverware glistening.

"Everything is perfect, stop fretting," Hannah said, coming to stand beside her. By her friend's flushed cheeks, she too needed to expend nervous energy.

"Should we go to the garden for a bit of fresh air before the first guests arrive?"

Arms intertwined, they did so, and indeed, the fresh air helped a bit. Before long, they heard voices as the first guests arrived.

Miles walked out to where they stood. He greeted each one with a polite bow of his head.

"My lord, I am surprised that you accepted our invitation," Felicity told him with a smile. "Everyone has heard about your reluctance to ever marry."

The lord was quite handsome, with deep dimples when he smiled and sparkling grey eyes. "I had to come. You are one of my dearest friend's sister. I must ensure whoever attempts to court you is worthy."

"Not another one," Felicity groaned. "At this rate, I will have more guardians than suitors."

Hannah giggled. "I do not have to fear such encumberments."

"I would not be so quick to think that, Miss Kerr," Miles told her friend. "You are Felicity's close friend, and therefore, we will also ensure your suitors are of good standing."

"Oh dear," Hannah said, her eyes rounding. She looked to Felicity in question.

"If my brother put you up to this, I must insist the lot of you do not interfere, or I will ask you to leave. Hannah requires a suitor."

"And what of you?" Miles asked, giving her a knowing look. Felicity looked to Hannah. Had Evan said something to his friend?

Henry Campbell suddenly walked out into the garden. "Ladies." A stark contrast to the lord, Henry was of a slenderer build. Felicity would describe him as beautiful, with long lashes, straight eyebrows, and clear blue eyes. Although he was quite masculine, it was curious that a man so attractive did not seem to be aware of it. Where Grant, Evan, and Miles used their looks to attract women, Henry seemed bothered by his.

"I must warn you," Miles said to his friend. "Miss Felicity has stated that if any of us interfere tonight, we will be thrown out."

Henry met her gaze for a moment and then looked to Hannah, whose cheeks brightened. "I promise to be on my best behavior."

Her mother appeared at the French doors, motioning for them to come inside. Once there, Felicity realized quite a few people had arrived. Two young women would join her and Hannah that night. One was Ivy Ross, Calum's sister, the other Louisa Kent, a young widow with a cheerful disposition and money of her own, who came as support for Felicity.

Miles, Henry, Grant, and Calum were the men present. That left only a couple more who were missing. Neither of the Macleod brothers had yet to arrive.

When the door opened, Richard Macleod appeared. He looked different than Felicity remembered. Although attractive, he looked so much older than she'd thought him to be. Then again, he was five years older than Evan, which meant he was thirty-nine.

After greeting her parents, he walked directly to her. "It has been a long time, Felicity. It is nice to see you."

He had a deep voice, and despite meeting her gaze, she felt as if he did not wish to be there.

"It has been years, Richard," Felicity replied. "I hear you spend most of your time working. Do you not like to socialize?"

When his lips curved, he looked more like the man she remembered.

"Allow me to introduce you to my friends whom you may not know." She walked with him to where Ivy and Louisa stood and introduced them. Louisa's expression turned to one of shock, and after a soft greeting, she walked away.

"You know each other?" Felicity asked.

Richard looked in the direction in which Louisa had gone. "Yes. We met once. I am unsure why she was surprised to see me. Perhaps has me confused with someone else."

"It could be," Felicity said, but it was obvious something had indeed occurred between Richard and Louisa.

After introducing Richard to Hannah, he spoke to them for a few moments and then went to speak to her father. It seemed they'd worked on several projects together, which did not surprise Felicity. She wondered if her father would come to have a working relationship with Evan as well.

Hopefully his working would mean it would be easier for her father to accept that indeed he had changed. Or was making an effort at least.

When the dinner bell rang, she went to the adjoining sitting room to search out Evan. It was getting late and he'd yet to arrive. Something was wrong.

She hurried to find Grant and pulled him away from Henry and Calum. "I have something to ask you."

"What is it, sister," Grant said. "We have to go to the dining room."

"Why is Evan not here?"

Grant's brow furrowed and he glanced around the room. "I do not know. He spoke about attending."

"Did you say something to him?"

"We spoke about his intentions and I informed him that I do not approve."

When Felicity gasped, several people looked in her direction. She narrowed her eyes and leaned close so only her brother could hear. "How could you? This was to be the first of many occasions he would use to prove his intention to be a different man. You ruined it."

She pushed past.

"Felicity." Grant caught up. "You must understand," he whispered. "I care for him, but he will have to prove himself."

Whirling to face him, Felicity smiled to ensure no one suspected how angry she really was. "How will he accomplish that if someone interferes each time?"

"Felicity, Grant?" Their mother walked up with an annoyed expression. "Everyone is to be seated." She motioned to the dining room.

Throughout dinner, while attempting to keep her end of the conversation with both Calum and Richard, Felicity kept looking to the empty chair that had been designated for Evan. It was not next to her because she did not wish to attract too much attention yet, but next to Hannah and with Grant on his other side.

Seeming to notice the empty chair, her mother motioned a servant, who removed it. No one seemed to take notice except Grant, who looked in her direction. Felicity narrowed her eyes at him.

After dinner, everyone went to the parlor where they could listen to the music or walk outside in the garden.

"Would you care to go for a walk?" Calum held out his arm and Felicity took it. They meandered outside until reaching a bench.

Both sat and smiled at each other awkwardly. Unable to garner interest in anyone, Felicity decided to treat each guest as if they were candidates for Hannah. "I do not believe we have coincided much during the Season," Felicity said.

"I have seen you several times; however, there hasn't been an opportunity to speak to you more than a passing word."

After a moment, she considered that he'd been at Sorcha Robertson's affair. "Ah yes, I do remember seeing you at a gathering just a week or so ago."

"I take it this event is your parents' idea," Calum stated.

"What makes you say that?" Felicity answered with a smile at his seeming to notice she was not particularly interested in anyone present.

"A hunch."

Felicity looked up. "You are quite astute, Mr. Ross. I should mingle, it is my event after all."

When they walked to where Miles stood speaking to Richard, Calum greeted the men with casual familiarity.

After a few moments, she left the trio to whatever they spoke about and searched out Hannah.

Her shy friend had a slight flush on her cheeks as she listened to a conversation between Grant and Miles. When she noticed Felicity, she excused herself and hurried over.

"Come with me. I need to get away for a moment." She grabbed Felicity's hand, and they hurried past the parlor and into the now empty dining room. Hannah let out a long breath. "I feel as if I am going to faint. Just allow me a moment."

"I understand," Felicity told her, motioning to a chair. "Take your time."

"This is harder than I expected. Mother keeps sending people to speak to me, as if I am some sort of dimwit."

Felicity became annoyed. Of anyone, Mrs. Kerr should know that her daughter was shy and would feel awkward at forced conversation.

"We can remain together. That way I can help when you feel a bit overwhelmed."

"Is something wrong?" Henry appeared at the doorway. "I

was sent to find you."

"Mother?"

Henry nodded, his gaze moving to a still sitting Hannah.

"She needs a bit of a break every so often." Felicity did not explain further; Henry seemed to understand.

He walked to her friend and lowered to look at her. "Go ahead, Felicity. I will sit here with Hannah until I am sure she is prepared to return and face the ongoings out there."

"Thank you," Hannah whispered in an awed tone.

Felicity gave Henry a warning look. It was obvious that Hannah could barely tear her eyes from him. If he hurt her in any way, she would personally see to his public hanging.

At the end of the evening, Felicity collapsed on the settee and fell sideways. It had been a success. Two men had asked to be invited for tea the following day. Her mother accepted invitations on her behalf as Felicity pretended not to hear.

"I have things to do tomorrow," she told her mother, who walked in with more energy than should be allowed.

"Richard is from a wonderful family, and I believe Calum Ross is in line for a title."

"Poo," Felicity replied. "Titles are boring."

"Be that as it may, it would be something wonderful for your children." Her mother smiled broadly. "Go get some rest. Tomorrow will be a busy day."

"I promised to visit Hannah in the morning. We have to…"

Her mother gave her a knowing look. "I understand. You have to go over every detail of the event. Just be sure to return in plenty of time to change for tea."

CHAPTER ELEVEN

"ARE YOU SURE your brother is up? This is very early for him." Hannah peered out the window as they neared Evan and Grant's home.

Felicity's heart sank at seeing a familiar carriage in front of the house. Her driver brought theirs to a stop behind where Sorcha Robertson's carriage was.

"This is most awkward," Hannah exclaimed. "Perhaps we should leave."

"Nonsense," Felicity replied. "Not only do I wish to confront Evan because he lied to me, I also want to apologize to Grant for looking out for me."

Just as they arrived at the door, it was opened by the butler and Sorcha emerged. Her eyes widened at seeing Felicity.

"What are you doing here?" she asked with a sneer. "It is most disgraceful to chase after a man. Evan is indisposed at the moment."

Despite the situation, Felicity laughed. "Says the woman leaving a man's home." She rolled her eyes. "My brother lives here."

Sorcha obviously had no comeback, and without another word, swept past, bumping Felicity's shoulder.

"What a witch," Hannah exclaimed. That her friend said something like that made Felicity chuckle.

"If it wasn't that my heart is broken and I am so angry right now, I would demand a celebration at your newly found boldness."

Grant came to the door; obviously the butler had summoned him. With his hair pointed in every direction and crookedly buttoned shirt, it was obvious Sorcha had awakened him.

"I must speak to you," Felicity said, walking into the house. "I think I owe you…" She looked around. "Where is Evan? I want to slap him."

"Get in line," Grant said. "You'll have to go to his place of work. He is not here."

"Oh." Felicity and Hannah exchanged looks. Sorcha had implied he was there to anger Felicity.

"Now what do you owe me because I am going back to bed. You can do what you wish. Just do not burn the house down. Sorcha already threatened to do that."

"Goodness," Hannah said, her hand on her throat.

"Mother expects you at the house at two o'clock sharp." Felicity motioned to Hannah and they walked back out.

"Interesting," Felicity said. "Sorcha seems a woman scorned."

"Do you think they…you know," Hannah began, "and that is why she is so upset?"

"Probably," Felicity said. "It is so unfair that men can do such things, have intimacy with different people. But we have to remain chaste and be without a clue upon our marriage night."

Hannah nodded. "I agree. It is not fair at all."

"My goodness," Felicity said. "You are surprising me today." The driver held the door open for them and they climbed into the carriage. "Where to, Miss?"

"Macleod Textiles, just drive by and then home."

"What do you plan to do?" Hannah asked. "Speak to him?"

"Goodness no. I want to see if Sorcha is bold enough to go there."

When they rode by, it was satisfying to see that the woman's carriage was nowhere to be seen.

BY ONE O'CLOCK, Felicity was dressed and ready to receive her callers. In a lilac gown with delicate yellow daisies embroidered at the sleeves and bodice, she stood by the French doors.

"Do you require anything else?" Ana asked.

"Is this not the most awkward way to meet a potential husband?" Felicity asked.

Ana smiled. "It is the way society does things. I think it is rather sweet. To meet and converse, share tea."

"Ha," Felicity chuckled. "You are such a romantic. I do appreciate that about you."

Gerard stood at the doorway. "Mister Macleod here to see you."

Felicity frowned. She didn't have a clue how to deal with Richard. Had he said something the night before and she'd forgotten?

"Yes, of course, show him in."

When Evan appeared, she let out sharp breath and looked at Ana, who smiled widely.

"Your invitation was for last night," Felicity said, annoyed that something in her stomach fluttered.

Evan neared. "I came to speak to your father."

"My father?"

"What is it, young man?" Her father appeared through the doorway, seeming disturbed at being taken away from his work.

"Alone," Evan said, and followed her father out of the room.

"Whatever is that about?" Felicity asked Ana, who shrugged.

Her mother rushed in. "What did you do now?"

"Nothing," Felicity replied. "Why do you always assume I did something?"

Just then Hannah walked in. "I heard."

"What is happening?"

To Hannah's consternation, everyone stared at her, waiting

to hear what she'd heard.

"It seems Lady Ross told Lachland not to call on you. Her maid was walking the dogs and spied you and Evan having a rather passionate moment in the garden here the other day. Calum asked Miles if you were always so free with your attentions toward men."

"Oh." Felicity fought to come up with a response.

"Felicity, how could you?" Her mother lowered to sit. "Whatever will we do when Richard arrives?"

"It's just a rumor."

Just then Grant arrived. By his murderous expression, he'd also heard.

"What exactly happened? Did Lady Ross stand at the corner and scream the rumor?" Felicity asked.

"Is that all it is?" Grant asked. "A rumor?"

"No, it is not." Evan entered the room.

When Grant's fist plowed into the side of Evan's face, he lifted his arms to defend himself, but did not hit Grant back. Grant punched Evan's midsection and he fell backwards and crashed against the wall, knocking a table over, a vase crashing and splintering into pieces.

Hannah, Ana, Felicity, and her mother all screamed and ran toward the French doors, but couldn't keep from turning to watch. Her father and Gerard rushed in to break up the fight. It was a struggle, as Grant was too angry to stop pummeling Evan.

By the time her father and Gerard managed to pull Grant away, Evan bled from the nose and lips.

Everyone was silent, without words to begin to explain what was happening.

"You will marry my sister," Grant said. "Immediately."

"I will not be forced into marriage…" Felicity began.

Her father made a slashing motion with his free hand; in the other, he grasped Evan's lapels. "Be quiet, Felicity. You will do as told."

Gerard, whose face was red from restraining Evan, released

him and looked to the doorway. "It seems Mr. Ross has arrived."

Everyone turned to see that indeed Calum stood at the doorway with an amused expression. "It seems I have interrupted a rather personal exchange. I will see myself out." He turned and walked away.

"Go see about him and ensure he will not speak of this," Felicity's mother told her husband. "Hurry."

While her father went after Calum, Felicity and Hannah exchanged wide-eyed looks.

"Sit down, all of you." Her mother's tone left no doubt she was furious. She went to stand in front of Felicity. "I am so disappointed in you, young lady. To be kissing in public is most disgraceful, and to do it twice?"

"Twice?" Grant stared incredulously at Evan. Her brother furrowed his brow, obviously trying to figure out when the first time was that they could have been seen.

"Oh stop pretending," her mother looked first at Felicity and then Evan. "I saw you in the garden at Sorcha Robertson's dinner party. I was looking for Felicity."

Before Grant could do anything, she turned to him. "And you should be more aware of what your close friend is doing. My goodness, anyone with eyes can see they are besotted with each other."

Evan looked at Felicity, the corner of his now swollen lip twitching with restrained mirth.

Her mother tapped her foot, her eyes boring into Evan's. "As a gentleman, which I hope you are, I expect that you will do what you can to correct this matter. And that you will be faithful to my daughter. Otherwise, I cannot be held responsible for what I will do to you."

"Mother!" Felicity exclaimed as Evan's eyes locked onto her mother's curled hands.

"I have begun to make changes in my life to ensure it," he replied, and walked to where Felicity sat. He lowered to one knee. "Felicity Murray, I hold you in the highest esteem and ask that you do me the honor of becoming my wife."

She restrained from wiping the trickle of blood from the cut on his lip. "Are you absolutely sure?"

His face softened. "More than anything in my entire life."

"Then my answer is yes." Not caring that everyone looked on, Felicity threw her arms around his neck and kissed him soundly on the mouth.

"Goodness," Hannah exclaimed, and then giggled.

Her father cleared his throat, and her mother covered her cheeks with both hands and smiled.

"Ouch," Evan whispered.

Someone handed her a handkerchief, and she wiped his mouth before wiping hers.

Evan stood and turned to her father. "I just asked your father for your hand. He was considering it."

"I just hope you are prepared to deal with the spirited lass," her father muttered, seeming both perplexed and relieved at the same time.

Felicity started to argue at being called spirited, but decided it was best to remain silent at the moment. Her heart was beating wildly at the realization she was to marry Evan, the man she loved with all her heart. However it came about didn't matter at the time. All she could think was that he would be forever hers.

When Evan turned to Grant, her brother frowned and had crossed his arms. "What?"

"I hope we are still friends, especially now that we are to be brothers," Evan told him.

Her brother let out a sigh and held out his hand. "I am stuck with you then."

Evan slapped Grant's hand away and hugged him instead.

"I suppose we should celebrate then," her father said, shaking his head. "Young people can be so impetuous."

Her mother went to her husband and slipped her arm through his. "I most definitely agree. In our day, we would never dare. Gerard, would you please alert the others and ask that they bring champagne and flutes?" her mother instructed the butler, who hurried away.

When Gerard returned with Ana and two other servants, everyone held up a flute of sparkling liquid. Her father met her gaze and then Evan's. "To Evan and Felicity. We wish you good fortune and happiness."

As they sipped, Felicity looked at everyone around the room past her hazy, teary eyes. Everyone smiled brightly, excited to be the first to celebrate the happy occasion.

Bruising began to show on Evan's face, with a cut lip and another one above his right eyebrow.

"The both of you require cool compresses," Mae, the cook, said as she motioned to both men. "Please join me in the kitchen." Like repentant schoolboys, they followed her as she walked away.

"This has certainly been a strange afternoon," Hannah said, lowering to a settee.

Felicity looked to her friend. "Did no one call on you today?"

Hannah shrugged. "I did not expect anyone to. The only gentlemen who spoke to me were our self-appointed guardians, Henry Campbell, your brother, and Lord Johnstone."

"I am certainly disappointed," Felicity said just as Gerard reappeared.

"Mr. Campbell is here."

Henry walked in and hesitated, his gaze going from the shattered vase to the champagne glasses, and lastly to Felicity and Hannah. "What did I miss?" Henry asked with a confused expression, looking to every person in the room.

"Evan proposed to Felicity," her mother replied while her father poured another glass and drank down the contents.

Finally, Henry seemed to gather his composure. "I came to speak to Grant."

"He and Evan are in the kitchen," Felicity said. "Mae is looking after their injuries."

Her parents placed their glasses down and walked out of the

room with Henry.

All strength left her body and Felicity could only sit and look straight ahead. "What is happening, Hannah? I feel as if this is a dream. Will I wake in the morning and find that Evan never asked me to marry him?"

Hannah giggled. "It is all very real, dear friend. You are to marry Evan after the most chaotic and yet romantic proposal ever."

A wide smile split her face as joy filled every inch of her being. "It is all real. I can barely believe it."

IT WAS ALMOST evening when everyone finally dispersed. The only one left was Evan, who asked Felicity's parents for permission to speak to her for a few moments.

While Ana sat discreetly near the fireplace, Evan and Felicity were in chairs on the opposite sides of the room.

"I am sorry for the way this came about. I was planning for a more formal proposal, something romantic," Evan explained.

"Tell me about it."

He shifted and smiled. "A carriage ride, flowers, and brandy."

"It sounds delightful. We can still do it. We must speak of setting a date. Your parents will be invited to dinner tomorrow night. I think it is best we've made the decision by then. Mother wants it to be soon, to take advantage of the perfect spring weather."

"Whatever you decide." Evan looked over toward Ana and then leaned forward and kissed her. It was a soft kiss, but enough to make Felicity breathless, her entire being overcome with happiness.

CHAPTER TWELVE

"YOU'RE GETTING MARRIED?" his father asked with a tone of surprise the following day at the offices. "The Murrays have invited us for dinner to discuss the nuptials."

Planning to inform his father that morning, Evan was shocked that he had already been informed and invited to dinner.

It was only the afternoon prior that the entire episode at the Murrays' had occurred. Perhaps Felicity's mother moved quickly to avoid too many rumors flying before the engagement was formally announced.

"I am," Evan said. "I'd hoped to be the one to inform you and Mother."

His father smiled. "Mrs. Murray sent a messenger over yesterday evening. It seems she wasted no time." He paused. "Which leads me to believe there must be a very strong reason for the urgency in this matter. Is the lass with child?"

"No. God no," Evan exclaimed. "I planned to ask for Felicity's hand in marriage. I wasn't aware someone had spied on us...kissing in her garden, and well, you know how gossips are."

"Indeed I do," his father replied. "What intrigues me is that you did not stop your brother from attending the dinner party. Mind you, he is not interested romantically in Felicity, but if he were, it would have been awkward."

It was always best to be honest. "I did not feel deserving of her. Still don't, if I am to be honest. However, after realizing that I could not withstand her marrying another, I went to ask for her hand."

Robert Macleod studied Evan for a long moment. "You have always been headstrong and impulsive. By you taking a step back before deciding what to do along with the changes I've seen in you lately, I can state with assurance that you are more than worthy of the beautiful lass."

His father's words meant more than his own weight in gold. It was hard to swallow past the lump that formed in his throat, but he managed.

"I cannot express how much those words mean to me. This raises another subject I must discuss with you. I will not be able to come up with my portion for the sponsorship. I am sure that Henry, Miles, and Grant will pay their parts. Will you be able to find a sponsor for the remaining portion?"

"How do you propose to support Felicity?"

"With what I earn here. As I have stated, the monthly stipend I receive from my tobacco investment is enough to maintain the small staff. I will pay for the other necessities from my salary. I do receive one, don't I?"

His father chuckled. "Aye, you do. As a matter of fact, you are owed for this month. I think you will find that it will afford you a comfortable living."

Relieved, Evan closed the distance between him and his father and hugged him. It was the first time he'd touched him in so many years that he could not keep a tear from trickling down his cheek. "I am so very sorry for all I did to disappoint you, Father."

His father cleared his throat, obviously as affected. "You have returned to me, and that is all that matters. Let us leave the past behind."

Holding Evan's face, Robert Macleod pressed a kiss to Evan's forehead. "Now get to work and earn your pay. We cannot waste time having tea." He motioned to the door. "I will see you at dinner tonight."

"IT IS THE perfect day for a carriage ride," Felicity exclaimed, sitting beside Evan later that day. He'd had to hurry after work to ensure not to pick her up too late. When he'd met her at the door of her house, she'd given him a shy smile, lifting her face for him to kiss her cheek. "We do not have much time, dinner is in a pair of hours." She'd placed her hand in the crook of his arm and he'd led her to the open carriage.

Now, as the light breeze blew across their faces, Evan wondered why he'd never done something like this before. The driver went slowly, taking them through a wooded park where people often went for leisurely rides.

While Ana stitched, doing her best to remain unintrusive, Felicity smiled widely, looking around at the passing scenery. "I have not been through here in years. When I was very young, my mother would bring Grant and me here while our governess taught us about the foliage and trees. I did not find it as enjoyable as today. Today, I find the surroundings enchanting."

"It is beautiful," Evan agreed, and pressed a kiss to her temple. "However, I must admit to finding you much more enchanting. I have never been here."

"Never?" Felicity's eyes widened. "I thought all men brought women they courted here."

At the words, he considered for a long moment that he'd never felt strongly about anyone. Not anything like he felt for Felicity.

"That must be it," he finally said, meeting her gaze. "I have never courted a woman before."

Both women stared at him as if a third eye had magically formed on his forehead. Ana gave up pretense of not listening, and Felicity waited for what he'd say.

"I am not stating that I've not spent time with a few. What I am stating is that I have not courted anyone for any kind of long-term relationship." He felt the need to explain further. "And just to be clear, I have a reputation of being a rogue and I deserve it, but I never truly cared for another like I do for you. I have never been in love."

Ana cleared her throat and returned to her stitching while Felicity watched him for a moment. "I truly do not understand how that can be. However, I do believe you."

A carriage approached and their driver pulled to the left side of the path to allow them past. To his annoyance, it was Sorcha and another woman out for a ride. The woman's eyes narrowed as they rode past, and he hoped Felicity didn't notice.

His hopes were dashed when he looked at his fiancée. Her brows were lowered, and arms crossed over her chest. "Leave it up to her to ruin the afternoon."

"Do not allow her to." He wrapped his arm around her shoulders and pulled her closer. "Do you remember the names of the trees we ride past?"

It was endearing as Felicity did her best to impress him, concentrating on the passing foliage and naming each one with what he assumed was precision. Soon both he and Ana joined in the game of naming things first, at times dissolving into laughter when all three made up names.

They returned to a brightly lit house. Grant was already there. Although his friend had accepted his apologies, he remained a bit reserved and studied his sister intently when she was with him.

Evan didn't blame him. His friend made sure his sister was indeed happy and that Evan would give her a good life.

Felicity went upstairs to change, and Evan joined both Grant and Mr. Murray in the library.

"I spoke to my father today," Evan started as Grant poured whiskey. "He assures me that with my salary, I will be able to provide comfortably for Felicity. She will not want for anything."

Mr. Murray nodded with approval. "I am glad to hear it."

Grant drank from his glass. "I would expect nothing less. My sister will be well provided for, I'm sure."

Dinner was a flurry of good food, toasts, and both mothers bursting into tears several times while the men exchanged amused looks. Throughout, Felicity beamed, and Evan hoped to keep that amount of happiness on her face.

As the evening flowed, Grant could scarcely believe the turn life had taken and how unbelievably full his heart felt. That night, he would journal everything so that when he was old, he could recount the evening with Felicity.

Finally, they set the wedding date for the first Saturday in April, just a pair of weeks to prepare everything.

Evan considered that he'd not thought about the fact he would have to tell his friends that he could not provide his portion. At the last minute, he'd not been able to ask his father for the money. It was best to allow another investor to make the profit rather than borrow from his salary and attempt to live on less.

He would not tell them yet. Instead, he would wait and allow them to continue to find a way to fund their portions. There was a chance, albeit small, that he could still come up with the capital. Perhaps speak to his accountant and find out if he could get a larger share of the tobacco profits.

There was still nine weeks until the ship would sail. They had the rest of March and the entirety of April and May.

THAT NIGHT, HE arrived home tired, a bit lightheaded, but happy. Norman shook his hand, congratulating him as the two women of his staff stood by with wide grins.

Despite looking forward to his bed, he asked that champagne be poured, and he lifted his glass as Norman toasted to his upcoming marriage.

"Miss Murray and I will be married on the first Saturday in April. Of course I expect all of you to be in attendance."

"Will she come to live here?" Rosalie asked, her eyes sparkling with anticipation of having a lady oversee the home.

"Yes, she will. As will her companion, Ana, whom I know you have all met," Evan replied.

He considered for a moment that he kept the largest bedroom, and therefore, Felicity would join him there. "I do ask that the sitting room adjoining my bedroom be refreshed. Since she and Mother are redecorating most of the house, I will specifically ask they do not touch that room. I will have it decorated separately for Miss Murray."

"What of Mr. Murray?" Norman asked. "Will he continue to live here?"

"Yes, he will," Evan replied. "Now, I must find my bed. Thank you all for the good wishes. Please take tomorrow off and enjoy yourselves as a gift from me. There is much work to come."

The women looked to Norman, who nodded in agreement. Then with wide smiles, hurried away to conclude any chores so they could be free the next day.

"Thank you, sir," Norman said. "Good night, sir."

"Good night, Norman."

When Evan woke, it was clearly late in the day. It was a Saturday, which meant he was not expected at the warehouse.

He planned to visit Felicity later that day. However, first he would meet with someone about the redesign of the sitting room. He'd made an appointment to meet with the accountant on Monday, so he wanted to organize his papers and review his ledgers prior. Finally, he planned to meet with Henry at Walker's that evening.

When he went downstairs, he remembered the servants had the day off. Norman and the women lived in an adjoining wing that was behind the house. They had a separate kitchen and sitting room, so he would not see them that day.

"Where the bloody hell is everyone?" Grant grumbled, sitting at the dining room table with what looked to be a glass of wine.

"Are you drinking wine?" Evan asked with a smirk.

"What else is there? I cannot very well make tea without hot water." His friend glared into his glass. "This is not a good way to start my day."

Evan walked past to the kitchen where he added wood to the stove and lit it, and then he filled up the kettle from water in a decanter and put it on the surface.

"When did you learn to do this?" Grant asked.

"While preparing for being completely destitute, I asked to be taught things like lighting a fire and preparing toast, eggs, and bacon."

After slicing some bacon, he added it to the pan. While it browned, he prepared tea for himself. Following suit, Grant did the same.

When the bacon was done, Evan removed it from the pan, poured the fat into a bowl that was used for it, and cracked four eggs onto the heated pan.

"Mind you, the eggs will probably have shells and the bacon may be burnt, but it will be edible." Motioning to a table, he pointed at bread and a cutting board. "Slice bread for toast. If you are hungry and expect to eat, you must help."

Not too much later, they ate their breakfast.

"This is delicious," Grant exclaimed between bites. "I must compliment you on the seasoning. The cracked black pepper makes a huge difference."

Evan devoured his meal and reached for another slice of toast. "Father always asks for it, and I must admit, it does add a certain flavor that enhances."

He could tell there was something on Grant's mind. He studied his friend's still bruised face and almost chuckled. Grant's eye had turned a dreadful shade of purple.

"What are you looking at?"

"Your eye."

Grant's eyes narrowed. "You are not exactly in pristine condition." He hesitated. "Would you like me to move out?"

So that was what bothered Grant.

"Of course not. This house is huge. There is plenty of room for your entire family to come and live here."

"God, man, why would you say that?" Grant's eyes widened and he performed the sign of the cross. "The last thing I'd want would be to live with them again."

Evan had to laugh. "Very well, I will not invite them to move in. I promise."

They discussed what they planned for that day, and Grant admitted he'd planned to look for a place to live if Evan wished him to move out. Since he didn't have to, he invited himself along to speak to a designer about Felicity's sitting room.

It was late morning by the time they left. Evan insisted they wash up the dishes and pans so that the servants would not come back to a complete mess. Grant went along, although it was entertaining when neither were quite sure how to go about it. In the end, they managed and gained respect for what the women accomplished daily.

"I am not sure Madam LaGrange will want to take on such a small job," Grant said as they climbed out of the carriage at the elite designer's shop.

Although the woman who let them in seemed surprised, she quickly offered them tea, which they declined, and she hurried to inform her mistress of their presence.

Madame LaGrange emerged from the back room, a furrow between her brows instantly disappearing at seeing them. "It is rare for a handsome, much less two handsome men to visit my humble shop."

The designer's shop was anything but humble. Plush drapes on every window, thick rugs on the floor, and ornate chairs that she motioned to. "Please sit. Eliza, bring tea and shortbread."

This time, they were not given the option of declining. The woman lowered to a chair and they followed suit.

After discussing what exactly Evan wished and informing her that this was to be a gift and only one room, Madame LaGrange became animated.

"Am I to understand that you will finally marry?" Her face brightened with excitement. "The infamous Evan Macleod is to be wed." Her voice held a tone of awe.

Evan nodded. "I beg you to keep the secret until the engagement is announced next week."

"Of course. Of course." Madam LaGrange all but clapped. "I feel so very privileged to be one of the first to know. I will take the job. Once the new lady of the house sees it, she will demand the entirety be done. I am confident."

Exchanging looks with Grant, he hoped it would not be so as the woman was very expensive. She agreed to come to the house once she came up with a design.

"The price was not as high as I expected," Evan admitted.

Grant shrugged. "Perhaps because of the fact that she is ahead of the gossips with the news of your marriage."

"I should consider how else the announcement could benefit me financially," Evan said with a chuckle. "Unfortunately, nothing comes to mind."

"I wonder," Grant said, "if my sister will manage to keep the secret. She is most ill-disciplined and oftentimes slips at keeping secrets. I am willing to bet she is at the modiste attempting to figure out how to order a dress for the engagement party without saying exactly what it's for."

CHAPTER THIRTEEN

THE MODISTE HELD up a mauve-colored fabric to Felicity's face. "I think this shade suits you," she said with a bright smile.

Already exhausted by the fact her mother kept finding fault in every choice, Felicity nodded. "Let's use this one."

Her mother's brow pinched. "How about a bright shade of pink?"

"Pink?" Felicity turned to her mother. "That color is too childish."

Thankfully, the modiste was trained and understood that her mother needed soothing for whatever bothered her. "Let us go to the back room. I have some new fabrics that just came in. Why don't I pour you another cup of tea..."

Felicity remained in the front room. She walked to where a newly created dress was hung. It was quite bright, bordering on garish.

"That is mine." Sorcha had entered while she studied the dress.

Her stomach flipped. The only person who could dampen her mood was this horrid woman. Felicity forced a neutral expression. "The color is too bright for my taste."

"Of course. You probably prefer something more virginal." Sorcha ran her hand along the bolts of fabric on the shelves. "I suppose I should warn you of why Evan and I went our separate ways."

"I do not care to hear it." Felicity looked toward the back room, willing her mother and the seamstress to return.

"I will tell you anyway," Sorcha said, closing the distance between them. "I would not give him the money he wants for that venture he and his friends are about to embark upon. They will lose all of it, of course."

The fact Felicity suspected her brother, Evan, and the other two were indeed planning something made her listen.

"That is why," Sorcha continued, "he decided it would be easier to marry and therefore have access to a dowry for the capital. I suppose it's an easy way to come about the money. Any young wit will throw money at Evan in an attempt to tame the handsome rogue."

Despite herself, Felicity's stomach sank. Surely if that was the case, Grant would not agree to it.

"Don't be so sad, the nights he spends with you will be most enjoyable. It will be worth your investment." The vile woman looked to the back room. "I suppose I will return later, I have much to do. Perhaps plan a dinner party in honor of my newly acquired freedom."

She rushed from the room, leaving a heavy scent of whatever floral perfume she wore. Felicity held out a hand to steady herself and let out a long breath. It couldn't possibly be true. If Evan planned such a thing, she would thwart his plans.

First thing upon returning, she would ask her father to withhold the dowry for a few months. He would agree when she explained that despite loving Evan, she wanted to be sure he had indeed truly changed and planned to support her without help from them.

She sank into a chair and realized she was clutching onto a burgundy fabric. The dark shade was beautiful, but not at all for a happy occasion like an engagement. And yet, it mirrored her state of mind perfectly.

"YOU HAVE BARELY spoken since leaving the seamstress," her mother said with a worried look. "I am sorry I was so picky. In truth, I was fighting not to burst into tears."

"Why?" Felicity took her mother's hand as a tear rolled down her cheek. "Please don't cry, Mother."

"It will not be the same once you marry. We will not have tea and toast every morning and discuss our day ahead."

The carriage rambled slowly down the street and Felicity considered it would be one of the last times she and her mother would do things like this regularly. "We will continue to be as close as ever. Spend time doing things."

Her mother smiled. "I know, darling."

When they walked into the florist, wonderful scents assaulted, and Felicity inhaled deeply. Her mother held up a bouquet of tiny white roses. "How delightful."

She leaned closer and sniffed. "A very light fragrance. I love it."

A misting in her eyes made her turn away to face intricately arranged displays and she sniffed. It was such a beautiful moment that Felicity could scarcely keep her emotions under control.

TWO WEEKS SPED by, and before she knew it, the morning of her wedding had arrived. Of course there had been a great deal of speculation by people about the haste of the wedding. Felicity didn't care. She was prepared to be wed to Evan and for him to find out about the lack of dowry.

Each time she'd tried to bring up the subject of what the men planned for an investment, Evan brushed it off as nothing that included him any longer. He refused to speak about it other than to say it was all resolved.

The fact he seemed not worried about his portion made what Sorcha said more believable. Several times, Felicity considered canceling the wedding. But she could not bring herself to bring even more curious speculation to her parents.

Her mother burst into Felicity's bedroom. "It's your special day and I wish to make every moment extraordinary."

Ana entered with a tray. On it were three plates with sugared toast and jam. Another maid entered with a tea tray.

Along with Ana, she and her mother sat at a table near the large bedroom window that overlooked the garden.

"Mother, why did you wish for our wedding to be so soon?" Felicity asked suddenly in contemplation.

Her mother shrugged. "I have to admit that I hate prolonging things, and the fact that some wait for many months, even a year, to plan a wedding is ridiculous. It gives time for much to happen between the couple."

At that last sentence, Felicity and Ana exchanged a look. "Is that what happened in your case, Mother?"

"This is not about me, it is your day." Her mother avoided eye contact, but not before Felicity caught a mischievous twinkle. Apparently, her parents had barely been able to wait to be together.

After breakfast, Felicity lingered in her bath, having to be prodded to get out so that a woman hired to do her hair could begin work. The style was an upsweep with ringlets at her temples.

When the hairdresser left, Felicity remained alone in her bedchamber for a few moments. She was to wear her mother's gown, a beautiful creation that Felicity had admired since a girl. Despite its age, the gown remained in pristine condition. It had long lace sleeves that tapered at the wrists and matching bodice that had been embroidered with pearls. With a cinched waist that would showcase her slim middle, the dress flowed out from the hips to fall in a cascade of silk and lace.

Sitting in a chair in her chemise, she studied the dress for a bit longer, admiring the intricate design of the lace, a pattern of flowers and vines.

Upon hearing voices, Felicity went to the balcony and peered down. In the garden, a group of women that were there to help sipped tea and chatted; their gay conversation floated up. It was amazing that her mother could throw a proper wedding together in a matter of days.

"It's time to get dressed." Her mother appeared, her overly bright eyes shiny with tears that threatened to spill.

"Don't," Felicity said as tears trickled down her cheeks. "I cannot show up at the church with swollen eyes."

They hugged, sniffing, and then burst into laughter when a crying Ana hurried in with handkerchiefs in each hand. "Stop at once."

THE CANDLELIT ROOM at the top floor of the Grand Central hotel overseeing the beautiful pleasure gardens that had been recently opened to the public was resplendent. Felicity had never seen something so breathtaking as the plush suite she and Evan were to share.

He poured brandy, meeting her gaze as he held out the small crystal glass. "Are you happy?"

Admittedly, at the moment, she was more nervous than anything. During the wedding ceremony, which was now a total blur, her emotions had run the gamut from happy, to worried, to nervous.

Her gaze followed the lowering of the fabric when Evan removed his coat, folded it, and draped it over the back of a chair.

She was curious to what would happen between them that night, while at the same time, trying to decide when to ask him about what Sorcha had said.

"What is happening in that beautiful head of yours?" Evan

neared and touched his glass to hers.

They drank, and it being her third glass of brandy, it immediately warmed her from the inside out. Tomorrow, she would inform him of her request that he not receive her dowry. Today, she'd not let anyone, especially Sorcha, ruin anything.

"I am considering what you look like bereft of clothing," Felicity stated. It was true. Since they'd walked into the splendid room, she'd begun undressing her new husband in her mind.

"Is that so?" Evan's lips curved. "You will find out very soon. First, let us toast." He held up the glass. "To our happiness, complete honesty, and many years of joy."

Their gazes clashed at the same time as their glasses. The toast shook Felicity. Why had he included honesty? It was strange.

She sipped the brandy only to have the glass removed from her lips and replaced with his. His mouth took her with familiarity, and yet it felt so very different because this night would end with intimacy.

When his lips trailed down the side of her face to her neck, Felicity clung to him, her legs threatening to give out.

The heady combination of his kisses and very masculine scent made her mind whirl.

"Oh, Evan," Felicity whispered only to let out a breath when his mouth traveled to the top of her breast.

He'd deftly undone some of the buttons that ran down her back, but the trail was long, so he turned her, his mouth never leaving her skin.

As he unbuttoned each pearl, the coolness of the air caressed her skin. Felicity kept her eyes closed, fascinated at the sensations something as simple as air stirred within her.

Finally, he'd unbuttoned enough of the fastenings that her dress slipped from her shoulders, helped further down by Evan until the beautiful creation pooled like a cloud at her feet.

He lifted her from it and carried her to the bed. He lowered Felicity to stand next to it.

"For each item you remove, you will be rewarded," he stated, a playful light in his eyes.

Unsure what exactly he planned, Felicity decided to test him. She bent, unfastened her right slipper, and slid her foot out.

He sat and removed his right shoe, then he looked to her other foot.

With a wide smile, she removed the other shoe and he followed suit.

"Interesting game you play, sir. Even with my dress removed, you are wearing less clothing than I am.

His right eyebrow lifted. "Is that so?"

She unfastened the ties to her petticoat and allowed it to fall to the floor, leaving her in a stay and silky shift.

He stood, removed his cravat, and threw it over his shoulder.

Next, she removed her stockings, and he did the same. Felicity laughed when he comically tossed them to the floor.

"I believe we are still completely covered. You have not fulfilled your curiosity as of yet." Evan gave her a challenging smile.

Felicity removed the stay, leaving her in only her shift. She began to wonder if indeed she wore more than he did.

Removing his britches revealed well-formed, strong muscular legs that made Felicity stare for a long time. She wasn't about to remove her one item of clothing remaining. It was far too immodest. At the same time, she had to admit not minding that Evan did.

He was a man, after all. They were not bound to the same strict rules as women.

"I will not remove another thing. You go first." Felicity crossed her arms, already feeling quite exposed.

Evan chuckled. "Very well." Meeting her gaze, he removed his shirt over his head, the lifting edge of the piece revealing more and more of his body. Felicity was riveted, unable to breathe much less move. His thighs were muscled, his hips slender. She swallowed past the sudden restriction in her throat at seeing his private area.

She was unable to keep from gawking at what looked quite different from what she'd expected. It was shaped like a sausage and it jutted straight out from his body. However did men manage to keep that part of them hidden?

Beneath the staff was what she could only describe as a soft sack of flesh. Felicity turned her head to the side to get a better view. That part of his body was quite interesting, if she were to be honest.

She trailed her gaze up from his sex to his stomach and up to his expansive chest. It lifted and lowered with each breath. There was a sprinkling of hair that went across his chest and down the center. The trail led her gaze straight back to the light patch of hair just above where she shouldn't be staring.

A thought occurred and she gasped. "Are you planning to put that in me?" She pointed at his thick member, which suddenly seemed to grow bigger.

Evan closed the distance. "Do you not find my body attractive?"

"I must admit, you are very well-formed. I apologize for my rudeness, but I could not stop looking. We are built so very different, you know?"

"I am aware." When he pulled her against his nakedness, a surge of heat traveled over her. Unable to figure out where to put her hands, she settled for his waist. Upon feeling the warm skin beneath her palms, she moved them to his shoulders. He was all warm, hard, muscular heat.

"You did not answer my question," she managed.

"Let us not worry about that right now," Evan replied, taking her mouth just as she was about to ask again.

When his tongued pushed past her lips, she forgot the question, much too taken by what happened in that very moment.

The last of her clothes slipped softly past her curves onto the floor without her noticing it until he lifted her and placed her on the bed.

"Look at me," Evan said, and she stared into his gaze. "Touch me wherever you wish. I am about to do just that."

Her husband came over her, his mouth and hands in places no other man would ever touch. Felicity lost all her inhibitions, wanting to do the same: to touch, to taste, and to feel every inch of him.

The moment his hand touched between her legs lifted the fog of delight for a moment. It was shocking that he was so bold, but when his fingers moved, slipping between the folds of her sex, once again, she lost all thought of what occurred. The only thing she could think of and feel were the wonderful sensations that sent her floating and gliding back down again and again.

Evan's body was magical, hard and perfect under her hands as she slid them up and down his back, unable to keep from pressing her lips to his throat and shoulders as he moved over her. Interesting that his sex gave so much pleasure as he moved against her, their bodies pressed together.

Heat blazed like an inferno between her legs, and she wondered if perhaps he'd do something to sate it.

Evan's fingers slid between her folds ever so slowly, each movement making her want more of him, more of whatever was to come.

The tip of his sex nudged at her entrance and Felicity parted her legs instinctively, knowing it was how they'd join. She nuzzled against his neck, enjoying how he managed to caress her body while entering her.

"Oh!" Reality was like a slap across the face as he thrust into her body and a sensation like that of being cut raced down her legs. "That hurts," Felicity screamed, and tried her best to push him off.

Evan froze, his member fully emerged inside her.

"Wait," he whispered, his hands holding her hips steady as he pressed kisses to her face.

"It's not hurting. So do not dare move. I will bite you." Without realizing it, Felicity dug her fingernails into his bottom. "I mean it."

"We cannot remain like this all night." Evan's jovial tone almost earned him a bite. "I promise that if I move, it will no longer hurt." He pressed his lips over hers and whispered, "Relax."

Ana had warned her that the first time with her husband would be a bit uncomfortable. Her mother had insinuated that she needed to trust Evan. Neither had said it would hurt or that he would sink his member into her body that way. She'd have choice words...

Her thoughts evaporated as Evan began to move. He slid outward, not all the way, and then back into her. He repeated the motions several times until Felicity began to feel something.

She bit her lip.

"Stop thinking." Evan met her gaze. "Would you remove your nails from my flesh?"

"Sorry," Felicity said, noting he did not stop moving.

Closing her eyes, she let out a breath, doing her best to relax as he'd told her earlier. However, relaxing was the last thing she could do. Each movement made her senses leap to awareness. When his mouth closed over hers and his thumb circled the tip of her right breast, relaxing was the last thing she could do.

"More!" Felicity called out. "Oh yes." She never wanted him to stop, never. Evan was drenched in sweat, both of them slick with perspiration, and still Felicity did not want to ever stop. Something was cresting, and she would find out what it was.

"Bloody hell!" Evan called out between ragged breaths. He slid his hand between them and touched a part of her sex that sent her flying. Her body arched and she cried out.

"Oh God!"

What Evan did after she was not sure as she was somewhere in the sky, stars circling in her eyes, and then she began to float down just as he collapsed over her with a loud, throaty growl.

Evan fought to catch his breath. "You are to be the death of me. I have never gone this long before."

"Mm mm." Felicity was not about to leave the perfect place

of her body humming with delight and the delicious inability to breathe properly.

"Are you awake?" he asked, looming over her. "Felicity, did I hurt you?"

Frustrated that he would wish for her to return to the boring earthly realm, she opened her eyes. "What?"

"Did I hurt you?" he repeated.

"You said I was going to kill you. It seems you are the one who is hurt." She lifted to her side and peered down his body. His sex was broken. It had deflated and now rested on his thigh.

"Oh no!" she exclaimed, and patted it cautiously. "Are you hurt?"

Evan began laughing and did not stop until tears rolled down his cheeks.

CHAPTER FOURTEEN

THREE DAYS LATER, they attended breakfast at the Macleod's. Mrs. Macleod insisted on having them, as well as several of their closest family friends, to celebrate their wedding.

It was obvious that Lilian Macleod feared the rumors and hoped that by people seeing them, they'd be reassured the speedy wedding was more to keep the anxious couple from each other prior to the wedding and not because they'd already been together.

Besides her parents, Felicity recognized Lord and Lady Ross, Mrs. Middleton, and her husband. The Campbells, Henry's parents, were also in attendance.

They were greeted at the door by an austere butler whose face softened at seeing Evan. They walked into a cloud of floral scents that mingled with the aroma of food and tea.

Both Mr. and Mrs. Macleod rushed to greet them. Her new mother-in-law threaded her arm through Felicity's. "You must come and greet our guests." She gave her a secretive smile. "How do you feel today?"

"Wonderful," Felicity exclaimed with so much enthusiasm that both Evan and his father cleared their throats.

In the sitting room, those in attendance looked at her with unveiled curiosity and Felicity held back the urge to stick her tongue out. Instead, she allowed the marital bliss to shine, and she smiled widely.

She went from person to person to accept congratulatory

greetings, her face beginning to hurt from smiling. Most were sincere, but it was obvious that both Mrs. Middleton and Lady Ross were not as much, their gazes moving ever so slowly to her stomach region.

Just then her mother and father arrived. She hurried over to hug them, as she'd not seen them since the wedding day.

"I so missed you, Mother," she said, kissing her matriarch's cheek. "I have so much to tell you."

"I am sure there will be a time, dear. Right now, we must ensure everyone here realizes you and Evan had a proper courtship."

They had not had a courtship at all that Felicity could recall. She gave her mother a quizzical look. "I do not think we did."

Her mother took her by the arm and pulled her to a far corner of the room. "What I mean to say is that you and he must ensure everyone is aware you were infatuated with one another but were not intimate prior to your wedding night."

"Oh." She shrugged. "It is really none of their business. I do not know why people are so nosy about things like that when people like Sorcha Robertson flaunt their lovers in plain—"

"Shhh!" Her mother let out a slow breath. "Please, Felicity, do try to behave."

Dinner was announced and they went to the dining room. There were stunning flower arrangements on the sideboards and short ones down the center of the beautifully set table.

Felicity found herself seated next to Lord Ross and across from Mrs. Middleton. The woman's expression was utter glee, either at acquiring fodder for gossip, or that she was about to eat. Felicity wasn't sure, as the rather rotund woman was obviously enamored with both.

"How do you find married life, dear?" she said once everyone began to eat.

"It has only been three days, Mrs. Middleton; I am not quite settled into it." Felicity sipped her wine.

The meddlesome woman slid a look across the table to Lady

Ross, who spoke to Mister Campbell. "I suppose it is so soon. Everything occurred rather quickly…"

"May I say," Lord Ross spoke over the din of conversation, meeting Felicity's gaze, "I was not aware you and Evan had married until my wife informed me of the reason for this dinner party. I am happy for you." The pleasant man gave her an approving nod. "Well on you."

Missus Campbell smiled at Evan when he whispered something into her ear. Evan met Felicity's gaze with what she could only gather was some sort of warning.

She leaned into her mother. "What is Evan about to do?"

"A toast?" Her mother stared across the table at Evan, who clinked his fork on the side of the glass.

He stood, and she could not tear her gaze away. Her husband was so very handsome, and she could not stop picturing him naked no matter how hard she tried not to. There had to be something wrong with her. How was it that she had become some sort of…what was the word? Wanton was too mild…

Her mother elbowed her and she once again paid attention to what Evan was saying.

"…speculation can run rampant in our circles, but I assure you, Felicity and I married quickly because neither of us wished for a long engagement. We wanted to be together as husband and wife as soon as possible, if I am to be painfully honest."

"Evan!" Mrs. Macleod called out. "That is a most inappropriate statement."

"It's true," Felicity said. "It is best to be blunt. Why cannot two people marry hastily if they wish?"

Everyone was stunned silent until Lord Ross held up his glass. "I thoroughly agree. Rules are for the weak of heart. Well on you, Evan."

Mr. Middleton and Henry's father lifted their glasses and joined Lord Ross in their agreement.

"It seems to be men against the women in this opinion," Mr. Macleod said, chuckling.

"I have to agree with Evan and Felicity," Henry's mother stated. "Long engagements are laborious."

The conversation floated over them as Felicity smiled at Evan. She was so very proud of him.

WHEN DINNER ADJOURNED, the women went to the parlor and the men to the study. Evan detested the smell of cigars, but accepted one when his father held one out to him.

Noting Felicity's father walked toward the garden, he followed him. The older man seemed to relish the fresh air.

He turned when hearing Evan walk outside. "I am not much of a social person. Although my work calls for being friendly with the men in there, I prefer one-on-one conversations."

"I came to avoid the cigar smoke," Evan admitted, looking at the one he held. "Have never liked the smell of it."

Mr. Murray nodded. "Ah."

They stood near one another, each in their own thoughts. Evan mused at how starry the sky was as he looked up.

"I must say." Mr. Murray interrupted his musing. "I do not know what to think of Felicity's request that I withhold her dowry. I meant to speak to you about it. Is there a reason for her not to trust you with the money?"

Evan pretended to know, although his mind flew in many directions attempting to figure it out. "As you are more than aware, your daughter is always up to something. She may wish me to do something specific with it."

His father-in-law shrugged. "How are you finding things at Macleod Textiles?"

"Very busy." Evan went on to tell him about the business and how it was growing by leaps and bounds. Soon they would have to purchase another warehouse and hire more workers.

"I am glad to hear it," Mr. Murray said. "That you are excited at how well the business is doing sets my mind at ease. It is obvious you are proud of your family's work."

Evan nodded. "Proud and remorseful that I waited so long to apologize and admit to my father that I had failed."

A faraway looked crossed Mr. Murray's face and Evan considered that Grant had the same bridge to cross. He started to speak, but his father-in-law spoke first.

"We should go inside. They will wonder what we are about."

Evan enjoyed spending time here, while at the same time, he was anxious to get Felicity alone. Why had she asked her father to keep the dowry from him? Despite the fact he had no plans for the money, it must have given his father-in-law a bad impression of him. Did Felicity not trust him?

He managed to make it through the evening, and it finally time came for them to take their leave so that the other guests could as well.

His beautiful bride beamed at him when he whispered in her ear that it was time to head home. Her gaze moved over him, and immediately he knew where her thoughts went.

To his utter dismay, he'd hoped to avoid bedsport for this night. She was insatiable and demanding in bed. It was during his attempts to satisfy her that he realized he was twelve years older and had never bedded someone so young.

If his friends knew of this, they would make fun for the rest of his life.

As soon as the carriage rolled from the house, Felicity climbed on Evan's lap. "Kiss me. I am tipsy and miss my husband's lips."

"Will your husband mind that I kiss you?" Evan asked, accepting her inexperienced but very enticing kiss. To his dismay, he became aroused, his member hardening despite himself.

He allowed the kiss to linger and slid his hands down her back. The layers of clothing usually bothersome now saved him from his wife's eager hands.

Felicity slid to sit beside him and began to unbutton his

breeches.

"What are you doing?" Evan asked, pushing her hands away. "We do not live that far.

Feeling like a prude, he took her hands and kissed them. "There is something we have to discuss."

"Oh?" Felicity gave him a questioning look. "Are you to teach me something new?" By the way she slurred her last word, it was obvious tonight was not the time to speak to her about the dowry. Instead, he nodded.

"Yes. I want you to lay back." He pushed her back against the carriage side. "Now place your legs over my shoulders."

She giggled. "What will you do?" Following his instruction, she lifted her legs, and he lowered his head under her skirts.

Moments later, Felicity was calling out his name as he licked between her legs while holding her plump bottom in his hands. By the time she cried out with her release, they'd arrived at their home.

The driver avoided looking at them while holding the carriage door open, and by his flushed appearance, Evan gathered he'd overheard every one of Felicity's exclamations. He had no doubt his wife's companion would be ravished that night.

He helped Felicity undress after sending Ana off to her husband. Thankfully, she was fast asleep by the time he lay beside her.

Evan studied her sleeping visage and considered the conversation they'd have the next day. She'd toasted to being honest and yet had held back a secret. If the minx was up to something, he would have to ensure she learned the lesson of no longer being able to act on every whim.

WHEN FELICITY WOKE, it was the first time Evan was not in bed next to her. She pulled the cord to get Ana, who appeared almost instantly with a tray of toast and tea.

"The downstairs is in such disarray," Ana complained. "The workers showed up very early to begin removing the wallpaper."

"Oh, I'd forgotten about that." Felicity slipped on a creamy yellow robe and went to sit in front of the mirror. "I must dress immediately. I have to go see Hannah. Is Evan downstairs?"

"He left very early this morning," Ana replied while pouring the tea.

Felicity frowned. Evan had not told her he planned to do anything that day. Then again, the night before had been a blur of activity and she'd drunk too much and barely remembered much. Other than the wonderful tryst in the carriage, she could not recall even going to bed.

Her cheeks grew hot. She'd not be able to look Ana's husband in the eye. Surely he'd overheard her. "Ana, did Evan take the carriage?"

"No, he left on horseback."

"I see." She let out a sigh. "I wonder if I should go visit Hannah or remain here and oversee things."

"There is little to oversee. All of the furniture has been moved from the parlor and sitting room. I believe once those two rooms are completed, the dining room will be done."

She let out a sigh. "I best go see Evan's mother then. She will know what has to be done now. I promised to have tea with Mother today as well."

In the back of her mind, Felicity could not stop thinking it strange for Evan to have left without waking her and letting her know where he went. Perhaps it was something she had to ensure to ask of him. It had only been a week since the wedding. Despite everything being hurried, she'd expected him to stay at home for at least a full seven days.

When Felicity arrived at her parents' home, her mother smiled and hugged her. "I was not sure if I should expect to see you here today."

They walked into the sitting room and tea was brought.

"I promised. Why would I not come?" Felicity asked.

Her mother smiled. "You were a bit lightheaded, and I thought you might wake with a headache. How are you?"

"Well. I slept rather soundly."

Her father walked past the doorway and then returned. He walked in and kissed her cheek. "Has Evan spoken to you about our conversation yesterday? I told him about your request that I withhold your dowry, and although he tried to feign knowing, it was obvious you had not informed him."

"What are you talking about?" Her mother's wide eyes flew from her husband to Felicity. "Why would you ask that of your father?"

"I have my reasons." Felicity began. "Sorcha Robertson..."

"If you do not trust Evan, then you should not have married him. I will not hear of this." Her mother's hand shook as she placed the teacup down. "Felicity...that is an insult of great proportions to your husband. I am not sure what to think."

"He did not seem angry on the ride home..." she replied, suddenly feeling guilty.

"Probably because you'd been drinking." Her mother blew out a calming breath. "It is time that you stop being so impulsive." Her father attempted to back out of the room, but her mother stopped him in his tracks. "The dowry is part of a marriage agreement."

"He stated not to want it at all. Insisted I was to either keep the money or give it to Felicity."

"Of course he said that. Evan's pride has been wounded," came her mother's sharp retort.

AFTER A LONG day of spending time with her mother, who spoke at length about the proper ways a wife should act, and then a full afternoon with her mother-in-law, who helped her set up a sitting place for company in the dining room until all the work was done in the others, Felicity was exhausted.

Alone with a glass of brandy, she looked around the crowded dining room.

A message from Evan let her know he'd be working until late and she face eating dinner alone.

Just as she was about to order food be brought, Grant arrived. He walked into the house, looking around at the disarray. "I take it the workers are done for the day?" he asked.

"Yes, they are almost done with the parlor. Once the room is complete, the new drapes and rugs will be installed."

Grant sat at the table, which had been shortened for the time being. "It will be a welcome sight to see all the changes."

"Grant," Felicity began. "Is there much that needs to be done to your side of the house?"

Her brother gave her a sly look. "A good friend of mine has made it her objective to redo those rooms."

Felicity huffed. "You must not allow it. It will give whoever it is the idea that you plan to settle with her."

"She would not expect that."

"Is she married?"

"No."

"Someone's grandmother?"

Grant laughed. "No. She is someone who does not wish to remarry since her very rich husband died."

"Your roguish ways must come to an end soon. You should marry, brother, start a family." She studied her handsome brother. With midnight black hair that was fashionably styled and bright green eyes like hers, he was always dressed impeccably. It was obvious that his benefactors ensured he was never without the latest fashions and plenty of pocket money, but at what price?

"My roguish ways, as you put it, dear sister, afford me a very comfortable and leisurely life. As a matter of fact, I will be leaving on a month-long expedition to Africa next week."

They were quiet while dinner was served. Cornish hens in a

lemony broth paired with fresh steamed peas and thinly sliced carrots.

"Have you spoken to Evan? I am not sure what to expect of his working hours. I would have thought him home by now."

Grant shrugged. "He rarely came home for dinner. The work is never-ending; it is hard for him to pull himself away at the end of the day. I find it amusing that after fighting it for so long he is now obsessed with work. I sincerely think Evan is enjoying working with his father and Richard tremendously."

"I am happy for it then," Felicity said. "Can I ask you something?"

"Yes, of course."

"Why were you, Miles, Henry, and Evan trying to come up with money?"

At the question, Grant frowned. "I will tell you only if you promise not to say a word to anyone." He went on to explain about the plan for the four of them to sponsor a ship that would in turn make them very rich.

"It is a worthy investment then?"

Grant nodded. "Yes, but unfortunately, Evan is no longer part of it. He told me just before the wedding that his father will probably take his portion as he will not be able to come up with the money."

Her stomach dipped. Evan did not plan to use her dowry. What Sorcha had said was a lie. One last attempt by the woman to ruin things for Evan.

The food was too delicious to waste, so she ate again. Then she gasped. "I wonder what Hannah is doing tomorrow."

"What are you going on about?" Grant watched her with narrowed eyes.

"Nothing really. I think I need her to go shopping with me. I have yet to purchase Evan a wedding gift." She gave her brother a bright smile. "Why does everyone think I'm always up to something?"

Grant chuckled. "You will never change."

CHAPTER FIFTEEN

E VAN ARRIVED HOME to a house that looked as if it had been attacked and ransacked. Thankfully, Norman, who held up a lantern, helped him traverse to the dining room, where Felicity sat by the fireplace, curled in a chair with a book on her lap.

"You are finally home," she said, then looked to Norman. "See that Mister Macleod is brought something to eat."

"Your meal has been kept warm, sir," Norman said as he dismissed himself.

Evan neared and kissed Felicity, her warm palm on his jaw soothing. "I missed you terribly, husband. It will be hard to spend the days without you for company."

"There seems to be plenty to keep you busy. You will not even notice I am gone." He lowered to sit next to her. "Tell me about your day."

"Let us to go the dining table so you can eat. We can talk while you have dinner. I am sure you are famished."

Evan nodded. "In truth, I am very hungry." They went to the table, where he sat on the end and she on his right. There was an eager expression about her that gave him pause. He hoped she did not plan to go to bed right away. He was not only hungry, but quite tired.

"What do you wish to discuss?" he asked as he began eating.

Her face became troubled. "I owe you an apology and beg your forgiveness for asking Father to withhold my dowry. It was very rude and insulting of me. I saw Sorcha at the seamstress, and she told me you were marrying me only for my dowry. To use it to pay for something. I was stupid enough to believe her. I am a ninny and deserve for you to be angry...no, furious with me. I will not be surprised if you refuse to speak to me for a few days and avoid me by working late. But I assure you, nothing would wound me more than your absence."

She finally took a shaky breath, a tear sliding down her face, and Evan wasn't sure what to say. He'd planned to have a stern talk with her, but it seemed she'd been thinking about her actions all day.

It occurred to him that he loved her and what had hurt more than anything was her distrust of him.

"Do you not trust me, Felicity?"

After a loud sniff, she nodded emphatically. "I do trust you, Evan, I promise. It is just that you and she were involved. And that she knew about an investment made me think you'd shared with her."

"I agree Sorcha is convincing when trying to get her way. I apologize for her coming to you like that. I did tell her I was saving money for an endeavor; however, I did not tell her what it was about. Either way, it was stupid of me." He pushed his empty plate away and stood. Holding out his hand, he waited for Felicity to take it. "Let us finish this discussion in bed. I am very tired."

HE COULD NOT keep his eyes from his beautiful bride as she finished undressing once Ana left. The fire in the fireplace cast a light that outlined her supple body through the sheer fabric of the nightgown, each delectable curve there for his viewing pleasure.

When she slipped into the bed, he pulled her closer and looked down at her. "I love you, Felicity Murray Macleod, with your impulsiveness and all."

Her eyes rounded. "It is the first time you admitted to loving me."

"Is it?" He gave her upper lip a playful nip. "I believe to have said it many times while making love."

Felicity gave him a rueful stare. "Everyone knows it doesn't count then."

"Where did you hear that?" He had to laugh. His wife would never allow boredom to overtake their relationship.

"I heard Grant make that statement once."

When she reached for his bottom and pulled him over her, he acquiesced and took her mouth.

Before long, he plunged into her heat, his entire body trembling with pure arousal as her sex wrapped around his member so tight he almost came immediately.

"Yes!" Felicity exclaimed while lifting her hips to take more of him.

Evan was lost, completely and utterly undone by his wife's mewls of ecstasy when he held on to the top of the headboard and plowed into her, driving as fast as he could.

"More, Evan, more," Felicity exclaimed. "It feels so very good."

He could not believe it. The more he gave, the more she wanted. It was a dream come true to have such a free spirit in bed.

He withdrew. "Turn on your stomach," he instructed, and she happily obliged, eager for whatever he would do next.

Lifting her bum, he slowly entered her from behind and Felicity looked over her shoulder at him with a wanton smile.

He could not take it, had to drive in fully. The sound of their bodies colliding and her throaty sounds as he thrust in and out had his body screaming for release.

Felicity had come once, but he knew she needed another climax to be fully sated. The lass pushed her bottom back to meet his strokes; it was a beautiful sight.

Still holding her hip with his left hand, he reached around with his right to touch her and stroked the tiny nub at the center of her sex.

She went stiff and cried out, climaxing so hard her body seemed to pull him further in. Evan's release sent him spinning as his heated seed burst from him. He was barely coherent enough to fall sideways onto the bed, bringing Felicity with him.

Evan could barely breathe, his body shuddering with the aftereffects. Unable to keep from it, he grabbed her hips and began moving again. At first slowly, but then frantically. He'd never experienced anything like it.

It was as if his body took on a life of its own.

In the fog, he could hear Felicity's cries. She clenched the bedding while meeting his thrusts. It went on until he thought his heart would burst. Finally, he came again, and with a growl, he bit her shoulder in a primal instinct to claim his woman.

They lay in the afterglow of their lovemaking, Evan barely able to move much less think.

Felicity rolled over and pressed kisses over his face. "I cannot wait for tomorrow night."

Evan couldn't help but laugh. "I fear I may need a couple days to recover."

THE NEXT DAY, Evan hurried into work. He was running late, as he'd enjoyed holding Felicity that morning and had lingered in bed.

Richard gave him a knowing look. "Haven't had much sleep lately, have you?"

"The burden of marrying a young lass," Evan replied with a sheepish grin. "What is the priority of the day?"

He made a point to leave early that day so that he could meet with the others to discuss their venture. Evan wondered at their reaction when he informed them his portion would be paid for by his father, and therefore, his father would be the one to profit from it.

In a way, he hated to miss the golden opportunity, but he planned to save as much as possible so that he could sponsor a different ship in the future. It could be a few years, but in the end, he figured it would happen.

The lobby at Walker's hotel was not as busy as usual since they chose a late afternoon time to meet, when most men were still at work.

Grant had asked and acquired a private room, where he and Miles were already seated, each with a whiskey in hand.

"I hear your house is in disarray?" Miles said, his ever-present heavy-lidded look in place.

After his drink was brought, Evan replied. "Yes, Mother and Felicity had begun a project to update things before the wedding. Now it looks as if a storm hit the interior."

He let out a long breath, enjoying the fact he was to spend time with his close friends. "How are you, Miles? Any new conquests? I will have to live the single life through you all now."

The lord's left shoulder rose and fell in a lazy shrug. "Nothing new really. I have had a few enjoyable occasions with Eloisa Mackinlay. She is most appreciative of my companionship and has a wonderful way of expressing it."

"Is that so?" Henry entered the room, a drink already in hand. He lowered to a chair and crossed his legs at the ankles, a picture of leisure. "I take your appreciative lover and raise you two quite enthusiastic sisters."

"Sisters?" Grant asked, his eyes pinning Henry. "I do not believe it."

"Twins in fact," Henry said, "one blonde, the other brunette."

Evan drank from his brandy, holding back laughter, as it was obvious Henry lied by the way he baited Grant.

"I must say," Miles said, getting Evan's attention, "you look happy. Settled."

"I feel as if I have a reason to get up in the morning. I am sure you understand, as I know you keep very busy with your estate and such." Evan gave his friend a curious look. "Is your father doing well? I heard he went on a long trip."

His friend adopted a concerned expression. "Yes, he is touring our lands in the West Indies. He has not said anything to me, but I sense his health is failing and he wished to return home one last time."

"I am sorry to hear it."

Henry finished describing what was surely an exaggeration of making love with the fictitious twins and both turned their attention to Evan.

"Not only do I miss our gatherings, but I wanted to ask about the progress towards each of you coming up with your portion of the capital required. Father asked and I told him I'd bring him up to date," Evan informed them.

The men exchanged looks, each waiting to see who would speak first. Finally, Miles repeated what he'd told Evan.

Henry spoke next. "I have several plans in motion. I do not foresee a problem coming up with my portion." His devilish smile left no question as to how he planned to acquire the capital.

Opposite to Henry, Grant was evasive. "I will have my portion, there is no question."

The time came for Evan to tell them how he'd not have his portion. In his mind, he'd gone over several times how he'd impart the news. Taking a drink, he was about to speak when the server walked in to ask if they required refills.

"Yes," Miles said. "I would like to purchase a bottle of your best whiskey to celebrate my friend's marriage."

Everyone nodded and the man hurried out and returned with a bottle of very expensive liquor, which he proceeded to pour.

They toasted, and Evan hated to impart the bad news. He let the warmth of the whiskey linger down his chest.

Grant held up his drink. "I am happy to say and admittedly jealous that one of us has the complete amount required for their portion."

He looked at Evan and, in that moment, Evan considered

that perhaps he'd explained his father paying his portion incorrectly. Had Grant misunderstood?

"Congratulations, Evan." Grant held up his glass. "My father is excited at the prospect that you are putting my sister's dowry to such good use."

It took a moment for the information to sink in. "What?"

"My sister told Father about your plans, and he is eager to see what happens. According to him, he trusts that with the profits, Felicity will never want for anything."

"Hear! Hear!" his friends exclaimed, toasting, and all seeming genuinely happy for him.

"I have to admit to not expecting to have my portion," Evan said. "I had asked my father to be your partner in my absence if I could not come up with the entire amount in time."

His heart felt light. Despite the fact that the dowry was rightfully his, Evan would pay back every single cent upon the return of the ship.

When Evan arrived home, he found Felicity in the newly finished sitting room. He walked in and looked around, appreciating the transformation of the space.

"Once the parlor is completed, you can invite your friends over here for drinks and whatever it is you usually did," Felicity said, motioning for him to join her. A table had been set up for them to dine, and he expected it meant the dining room and parlor were next on the list to be updated.

Closing the distance, he pressed a kiss to her lips.

She caressed his jawline and deepened the kiss. His wife, ever so eager. They pulled apart when Rosalie walked in to ask if they wished for anything.

"Your study will be the first room upstairs to be redecorated," Felicity said. "I suppose we will have to move to the other side of the house while all that takes place."

Evan took her hand and kissed her knuckles. "What do you think of having a sitting room adjacent to our room?"

For some reason, he became nervous at showing her the

room he had redecorated. What if she hated everything about it? With everything happening so soon, he'd not taken the time to get a woman's opinion on it. Other than Grant, who declared it "suitable," he'd been the only one to see it. He supposed he could have asked Rosalie.

"It would be lovely to have a room to spend time in," Felicity said. "Especially when I wish to remain upstairs if you have business visitors or such."

He considered it for a long moment. "I think I will have my study relocated downstairs. The empty sitting room on the opposite side of the entry. What do you think?"

A chuckle escaped. "It will be a perfect vantage point for when our children try to sneak in and out. You will be in your study and I in here."

"Children?" Evan's breath caught. Certainly it was too soon for her to be with child.

Felicity gave him a droll look. "Do not faint. I mean in the future when we decide to have children."

Obviously, she did not understand that they had little say in when children were created. However, it was a conversation he'd allow her mother or his to have with Felicity. Instead, he pulled her to stand. "I wish to thank you. Today, Grant told us about your request that your father release your dowry. I will use it for the investment but will repay every cent back to your father."

"My father does not need the money. He's had it in a trust my whole life. It was specifically set aside for when I married."

He wasn't sure what to think or do. "What if I return it to you then?"

"It was not mine in the first place. Evan, it is my wedding gift to you. Please accept it. I have nothing else to offer."

Pulling her close, he nuzzled her neck. "On the contrary, you minx. You are priceless to me."

"Evan!" Felicity exclaimed, her hands flying to cup his face. "You spoil me with such beautiful words."

"Come," he said, pulling her to the stairwell.

When she giggled, he turned. "It is not what you think. I have something to show you."

"Oh poo." Felicity pouted. "Can you show me bereft of clothes?"

Norman cleared his throat and Felicity turned, her cheeks turning pink. "Sorry, Norman, I did not know you were there."

The butler gave her an indulgent look. "I wanted to know if you'd like dinner served now?"

"Yes, in a few moments. Bring it upstairs, to the green room," Evan said with a wink and Norman nodded, hiding a smile when Felicity looked at him.

Before she could ask, Evan tugged her hand. "Hurry, dear."

They went to the door next to the bedroom and he motioned to it. "Go on inside."

"Rosalie told me it was a mess. Did you have it cleaned out? Or are we to decide about it now? I do not wish to look now; can we wait until after we eat?" She looked across the hall to where his study was. There was only one other room, and it was a lavatory. "Where is the green room?"

He pressed a kiss to her temple and pointed to the door next to their bedroom. "In there."

Quick as a hare, she threw the door open.

It was hard for Evan to see her expression as she took a step forward and held her hands up, covering most of her face. She walked to the large windows where a grouping of four chairs had been upholstered in a beautiful sage green. The drapes were velvet, the color of emeralds. There was a cream settee with intricately embroidered ivy on the back and cushion. In addition to a pair of tables, throw rugs, and plush pillows, there were several trinkets placed here and there that brought life to the room.

Over the fireplace, a painting of Felicity wearing the pale green dress she'd worn the first time he'd seen her upon her return from Edinburgh. The portrait reigned over the room. The artist had added a beautiful pearl and emerald necklace to decorate her neck with matching earrings.

When Felicity whirled to look at him, tears were streaming down her face. "I will never wish to leave. This room is absolutely breathtaking."

Once again, she turned from him and hurried from place to place to admire what Madam LaGrange had done. Watching her delight and expressions made the cost of the room more than worth it. He made a mental note to personally thank the designer.

"I love the painting. Where did you get the idea for the jewels I'm wearing in the portrait?" Felicity asked, coming to his side and leaning against him when he placed an arm around her waist.

"You are not a very good explorer if you missed the jewels. They are laying about here somewhere." Evan waved around the room nonchalantly.

Felicity flew to one ornamental box, finding it empty. She went to a larger one that was placed on a table next to the window.

"Oh my." Her hands trembled as she reached to touch the beautiful jewelry that had once belonged to his grandmother.

"It is from my parents. They feel, as the first daughter-in-law, you should have them."

When she crumpled to the floor, hands over her face, and began to sob, Evan hurried to her.

"What's wrong?" He carefully picked her up and carried her to a chair, positioning his crying wife on his lap.

Even with a pink nose and clumped lashes, she was a ravishing beauty. "I am so very happy and feel so overwhelmed with joy at this moment."

"If only I could keep you this happy every day," Evan said, then kissed her tear-streaked face. "Come now, let us sit at the table, dinner is about to arrive."

Still sniffing, she went and peered down at the emerald necklace and earrings and reverently closed the box. "I will treasure this moment and each item in this room dearly."

They talked about the progress of the house renovations and made plans to host a dinner party once it was all completed. He could not take his eyes from Felicity as she spoke in great detail about what she planned to serve and how the house would be decorated. Who would have thought that a simple conversation like this would make him deliriously happy?

It occurred to Evan that, despite having wasted years on unimportant pursuits and having lost his entire fortune, it was all worth it to have ended up in that moment.

"You are quiet all of a sudden," Felicity said studying him. "Am I boring you?"

"On the contrary. I was musing at how happy I am right now." Evan smiled at her, and she returned it with an impish grin.

Her gaze moved to the door that led to the bedroom. "I have to admit to enjoying being your wife more than I thought possible."

CHAPTER SIXTEEN

"**Y**OU ARE POSITIVELY beaming," Hannah said as they settled into a table at her father's tea shop. It was bustling with activity, and it made Felicity glad. Although Hannah's family would never recover from the fire, at least the small business was providing income.

A young woman brought a teapot, cups, and sweet scones on a tray and placed each item in front of them. She poured the tea and cream and then left.

Felicity lowered her voice, looking around to ensure no one overheard. "There is so much I want to share with you about married life. But I am not sure I should."

Her friend's wistful look made her heart squeeze. Not having a sister, Felicity loved her friend dearly. If only Hannah would find love like she had.

"You must absolutely share everything." Hannah sipped her tea. "I would think it is better to be prepared for such things."

"Indeed," Felicity said. "I am not sure why men have to be so much more informed than us. It is silly, in my opinion."

They were to spend the day shopping for a birthday gift for Hannah's mother, and then her friend wished to see the renovations. Felicity was excited that they'd spend the day together.

"I have missed our daily talks. I wish you lived closer," Hannah said with a frown. "I suppose you are not that far, but without a carriage during the day, I can only travel so far."

"You can always hire one; I will pay for it. As a matter of fact,

I insist. I want to spend time with you as often as possible."

Hannah laughed. "I am sure Evan would not agree to me being there daily, but we can have a standing day for tea and things, like today. Tell me a bit at least," her friend prodded.

Felicity lowered her voice. "I always wondered what was said when my parents exchanged looks. Often Mother's cheeks would turn pink. Father smiled as if holding a secret, and neither met my gaze. Now I know that they enjoyed time together the night before."

The noise of the tea shop enveloped them as Hannah considered what Felicity told her. "Nothing like that ever happens at my house. As a matter of fact, I wonder why they are married. My parents are friendly to one another, yes, but in a distant type of way. They do not share a bedroom, and most certainly, I have never seen them exchange any kind of secret look."

When Felicity considered it, she realized that in the years of knowing the Kerrs, she'd never once seen them near one another, or for that matter, speak to one another at any gathering.

"That is strange," she admitted. "Why do you think that is?"

Hannah looked toward the window, seeming to picture herself elsewhere. "One day, Father was in his cups, and he said something to Mother, and I overheard. It seemed that Mother had wished to join the convent and her family forced her to marry my father instead. And to make matters worse..." Hannah's voice was barely audible. "Father had been deeply in love with someone else."

"It was an arranged marriage then?" Felicity asked, also whispering.

"Yes," Hannah replied, once again returning her attention outdoors. "I must say, Mother has such a sweet personality, and despite things, she and father have given me a good upbringing."

"You will marry for love," Felicity pronounced, no longer whispering. "I will ensure it."

After finishing their tea, they walked across the street to the same antiquities shop that Felicity had sold the painting.

She hoped the man was not angry with her.

"Ladies, welcome." He greeted Hannah with a warm smile, but his eyes narrowed and the smile disappeared when meeting Felicity's gaze. "You did not inform me that the painting was created by Mrs. Sorcha Robertson," he said with an unreadable tone.

Felicity swallowed, managing a wide smile. "Oh, was it?"

"Yes, it was," the man said, and he let out a long breath. "It hangs over in the next room."

Despite herself, she looked in the direction, and sure enough, it was visible from the doorway, the garish colors sharply contrasting with the otherwise tasteful décor.

"I will never sell it," the man proclaimed.

"I am so sorry," Felicity said, tearing her gaze from the monstrosity. "I feel badly."

"Why?" the man said. "Because of it, Mrs. Robertson and I have gotten to know one another. She and I are making plans to travel to Spain and Europe for an extended period. I feel as if I owe you more than I paid."

The man's expression softened, and his gaze became unfocused.

Hannah and Felicity exchanged a look, neither wishing to picture the normally austere older man in a passionate moment.

"I am seeking a gift for my mother." Hannah grabbed Felicity's hand and pulled her to a room where small trinkets were displayed. "A box."

The man insisted on trailing behind them, informing Felicity of each and every time he and Sorcha had met because of the painting being there. How at first the woman had been insulted, but upon learning he would display it permanently, she'd been delighted.

It took over an hour to get out of the shop, both walking a bit away before dissolving into laugher.

"I hope that means that awful woman will be out of our lives for now," Felicity exclaimed. "I just cannot, however, picture her and Mr. Hollenbeck together."

Hannah nodded. "He is smitten."

As they rode toward Felicity and Evan's home, she caught sight of Evan's horse. It was tethered at a coffee shop that was popular for business meetings and such. Her eyes bulged when Evan and Sorcha walked out of the establishment.

Sorcha leaned in and touched his forearm. Evan did not seem to mind; he nodded in agreement about something she said.

"Stop!" Felicity exclaimed, hitting the top of the carriage with her parasol. The coachman slowly brought the carriage to the side of the road.

"What is it?" Hannah said, but then quieted and peered out the window with Felicity.

They watched as Evan walked Sorcha to her carriage, and then right there in plain daylight, she hugged him.

The coachman came to the door. "Is something the matter, Mrs. Macleod?"

Felicity ignored him, watching as Evan mounted and headed in the direction of his workplace. "Take us to Macleod Industries. I must speak to my husband."

The coachman looked in the direction of the coffee shop and nodded. Obviously, Ana's husband had also seen Evan. "Yes, of course, Madam."

They arrived just as Evan was dismounting. He turned at the sound of the carriage and smiled when noticing Felicity climb down. She'd not bothered to wait for the door to be opened for her.

"What has you in such a hurry…" He stopped talking because she slapped him hard across the face.

Her hand stung from the contact, and still she wanted to slap him again. Unfortunately, he caught her hand when she tried.

"What are you doing?" He looked genuinely perplexed.

"How dare you?" Felicity exclaimed as Hannah rushed to them only to stop a few feet away, unsure what to do.

Her gaze focused on the bright red mark her hand had left,

the coloring giving her only a bit of satisfaction.

"Felicity, I will not stand for such public displays—"

This time, she kicked him. "Public display?" she screamed. "You did not seem to mind the public display just now at the coffee shop."

He stilled. "Oh that."

"Do not come home tonight. I mean it, Evan. You best not come near me tonight." Felicity snatched her hand away and turned toward the carriage.

"It was nothing, Felicity. She was—"

"Stop it, do not make excuses." She was too angry to think clearly. All she wished at the moment was to get away from him. "I do not care to hear what that woman wanted. After all the rumors of her and you, how could you allow her to touch you in such a familiar manner in public? How could you do that to me?"

Her chest constricted and breathing became almost impossible.

"I best take her home," Hannah said, putting one arm around her, the other keeping Evan back. "Please. Give her some time."

"Felicity," Evan called out, but she shook her head and rushed back to the carriage. There was nothing he could say or do that would repair what people were in all probability murmuring about at the moment.

That he'd returned to his lover so soon after marrying. Whether it was true or not, the damage would linger. Not only had they hugged in public, but in all probability, lingered over coffee. A bitter drink she hated and now would detest forever.

Unable to see past the tears or hear because of how hard her heart thundered, Felicity wasn't aware where they went. Obviously, Hannah had spoken to the coachman because they traveled at a quick clip.

Moments later, they pulled up to her parents' home and Hannah held her by the arm as they went to the front door and past a surprised Gerard.

"I will alert your mother," he said, seeming to note her distress.

"What happened?" Her mother hurried into the sitting room and Hannah proceeded to tell her.

"Oh no!" her mother exclaimed. "I understand how you feel, but you should have never gone to his place of business and created a spectacle in public."

When she pulled Felicity into her arms, soothing her with "there-theres," Felicity wanted to linger, but at the same time, she was too angry to keep from standing and pacing. "How could he? How dare he?" she said to no one in particular. "I will be the laughingstock. Everyone will ponder that it did not take long for him to return to his last lover."

"And what about Mister Hollenbeck. No doubt he will hear about it shortly."

"Oh, Hannah," Felicity snapped. "No one is aware of their relationship, if one could even call it that. It seems Sorcha's affections change as often as the weather."

Her mother looked from her to Hannah. "Tell me, what did Mr. Hollenbeck say to you?"

Losing interest, Felicity could only continue to pace, fuming at what had transpired. Not only had Evan been seen in public with Sorcha, but then whoever happened to look from inside the windows at Macleod Textiles had witnessed her slapping and kicking Evan. What a mess. And it was entirely his fault.

Her mother insisted she drink strong tea with a bit of brandy, and she gulped it down, not caring that it was most unladylike. After this day, she'd left her manners behind.

Withing moments, her mother had come up with a plan for damage control and they headed back to same coffee shop where Evan had been.

A messenger had been dispatched with a note to her husband, in which Felicity had no idea what her mother had scribbled.

"Remember, head up and smile on your face. It has to seem as if whatever the rumors said about your actions earlier are not true." Her mother nudged her, and Felicity plastered a wide smile on her face.

They entered the establishment acting as if in the middle of a conversation. Hannah giggled a bit too loudly and Felicity's mother gave her a warning look.

It was obvious by the many heads turning that the last person anyone expected to be there was Felicity. She felt every single stare, almost flinching when someone across the room began speaking to her companion.

"Mother, I am so delighted you wished to come here today," she said, noting women at another table listened.

They began discussing plans for the house renovations, and despite her anger, she began to relax. The idea of how each room would be transformed was her pet project at the moment, and she was so enthralled by it that even after Evan's actions, her enthusiasm was only dimmed slightly.

It was obvious when Evan entered because the conversations lulled. He walked straight to the table and placed a kiss first to Felicity's cheek and then to her mother's. Finally, he lowered to the chair next to Felicity with the easygoing expression of a man without worry.

If not for the fact they were there to perform, she would have slid her chair away. Instead, she leaned into him. "Darling, I am so glad you stopped by. I had to ensure you agree to the wallpaper being removed from the parlor today."

"Whatever you ladies decide is best. I know nothing of these things." He shook his head when a server came to offer food or drink. "I am afraid I cannot stay. I came inside only because I saw our carriage out front."

With that, he stood, once again made a display of kissing her cheek, and walked out, his attractive figure catching the attention of everyone he passed. Other than nodding in acknowledgment at a man, he did not pay anyone else any heed.

"Now, should we discuss the dinner party?" her mother said, and once again, the busy-bodies at the nearby table seemed to lean in to hear.

It was an hour later that they walked out of the coffee shop, and to Felicity's relief, Hannah begged out of coming over to see what was being done.

Apparently, her friend was sensitive to her feelings and expected that Felicity preferred to be alone.

Norman greeted her at the door. "The men are almost finished with the parlor walls and paint. They will begin relocating furniture from the dining room in there."

"I will make myself scarce then and remain upstairs." Felicity turned to the stairs only to stop. "Norman, you know all that happens in this house; therefore, I must inform you that I am very angry with Mr. Macleod today. I am not sure if he will come home tonight. If he does, tell him I prefer he stay in Grant's side of the upstairs."

The butler's expression did not change. "Of course, Mrs. Macleod."

"Oh and no tea or dinner. I've eaten twice already and am very full."

She climbed the stairs, exhaustion seeming to pull on her legs. Instead of pouting in the bedroom, she went to the now christened Green Room and directly to the large windows. The room faced the side of the house, giving her a glimpse of the road leading up to the house, and in the distance, a view of the edges of Glasgow. She closed her eyes for a few moments, hoping to regain some semblance of control over her thoughts.

Why had Evan met with Sorcha? Was it possible they made some sort of agreement so that when she returned from her travels, they could be together again?

As much as she enjoyed bedsport, Felicity figured she was lacking in experience, which obviously Sorcha was well versed in.

The fear of being inadequate, which had followed her like a shadow all her life, surged until she had to take deep breaths and sit.

According to her mother, she was to allow Evan to explain. At the moment, she could not fathom even being in the same room with him.

Also, her mother insisted they make a public appearance at a social event. With everything they had to do, including the renovations on the house, the last thing Felicity wished to do was to waste time at an event where she barely knew any of the attendees.

However, there were two invitations on the table in the sitting room downstairs that she'd barely glanced at the night before.

One was for a large engagement party at an estate just outside of city limits. The other was a smaller spring soiree at an acquaintance's home. She would accept the second one.

It was not much later that she heard male voices echo through the house. Felicity went to the door and opened it to listen.

One of the speakers was Grant, the other Evan. It sounded as if Evan was mad because he spoke louder than Grant.

She didn't care that he was angry. Closing the door slowly, she turned the key and locked it, then she hurried to the bedroom and did the same. Tonight, she did not trust herself to be around Evan.

Three short raps on the door made her jump, and Felicity stared at the door without speaking.

"Felicity, open the door." It was Evan, his tone level, but there was no mistaking the edge to it.

When she didn't reply, he knocked again.

"I refuse to sleep anywhere other than our bed." Evan knocked on the door, this time harder. "Open the door and talk to me."

Moving closer, she blew out a breath. "I cannot speak to you right now. I am too angry. Go away."

"I understand your anger. I made a mistake."

Felicity climbed into the bed and pulled the blankets up over her ears. It seemed like only moments later that she woke when hearing a curse in the adjacent room. She sat up. How had someone gotten in there?

Just then Evan came in through the door, hair all over the place, dirty patches on his knees and out of breath. He stood in the moonlight staring at her.

"I cannot stand the idea of you being angry with me," he said, nearing the bed.

Felicity held both hands out. "Don't you dare come near me in that state. You are all dirty and sweaty. What have you been doing?"

"Climbing the bloody trellis. It broke and I fell, so then Norman came with a ladder." Sitting down, he pulled his boots off, followed by his breeches and shirt. "I need a bath."

Felicity watched him. "What do you plan to do now?"

"Wash up," he snapped, walking to the washstand. "You could have opened the door."

"Do not get petulant with me," Felicity told him. "You are the reason we find ourselves in a scandal. If not because you cannot stand to stay away from Sorcha R—"

"First of all," Evan said, turning to face her with a washcloth in hand. "She approached me as I was leaving the coffee shop. Informed me that she was leaving and wished to apologize for all she'd done. It was a quick farewell hug, nothing more."

"Everyone at the coffee shop stared at me when I walked in," Felicity exclaimed. "They saw what I saw."

"I think it had more to do with the fact that someone from that coffee shop had brought a delivery for our staff, which I had ordered, and arrived just as you slapped me."

Felicity considered that perhaps she should have waited for Evan to explain what happened before striking him. So it was she who had done the greater misdeed. Evan could not help that as he walked out, Sorcha had approached him.

"I would never do anything to hurt you or our marriage, you must believe me."

The fact that he stood totally naked, mussed hair and looking so contrite, made her heart explode with love for him. He was so utterly beautiful and powerful at the same time. Guilt assailed her at having been so impulsive and for hitting him. Felicity pushed the bedding aside and rushed to him. "I am so very sorry, Evan. Please forgive me. I am so very, very sorry." She peered up to his softened expression.

"Of course I forgive you." His reply was the sweetest sound.

Evan leaned forward and pressed his lips to hers, tentatively at first and then, to her delight, kissed her soundly, the entire time his hands traveling down her body. "You can make it up to me."

"How?" she whispered, excited at the idea of making love.

"I may have splinters in my hands and knees. Can you look?"

THE NEXT MORNING, Felicity stretched next to him, and Evan pulled her close. Once again, they'd made love until he could barely catch his breath. Even now, he was reluctant to move if it meant waking the minx and her wishing for a proper farewell before he left for work.

Slowly, he slid from the bed and managed to dress without waking her. Feeling triumphant, he started for the door.

"Evan?" Felicity called after him sleepily. "It is still early, come back to bed."

He smiled at the beauty indulgently and went to kiss her soundly. "I must go downstairs and find something to take. I have a bit of a headache."

"Oh." She gave him a soft look. "Yes, you see about that."

Smiling at his cunning, Evan walked down the stairs and found Grant was already awake. Next to him stood Henry. Both looked up at him with strange expressions.

"What happened?"

It was Henry who spoke. "I was riding home earlier, after leaving from a rather entertaining interlude. I happened by the Kerr tea house, the door was wide open, and it struck me as odd as all the lights were off."

"Where they robbed?" Evan asked, feeling badly for the already financially strapped family.

"No," Henry said. "I found Mr. Kerr on the floor dead. He's been murdered."

Instinctively, Evan looked up to the stairs. He would have to inform Felicity immediately. She would wish to be by her friend's side. "How long ago was this?"

"Just an hour or so. I spoke to the authorities, and they told me I was free to go. I am not sure, but thought perhaps Felicity could accompany me to speak to Hannah's family."

Evan turned and hurried up the stairs. "Yes. Of course."

It was not much later that he sat next to a stone-faced Felicity. She'd stopped asking Henry questions, seeming to acknowledge he'd have to answer the same ones over again once they arrived at Hannah's home.

The household didn't seem to be awake as of yet. The curtains on every window were drawn.

They walked to the front door and knocked. In the distance, Felicity caught sight of two men on horseback headed there. "I think they come to inform them as well."

The door was opened by a bright-eyed cook, who gave them a questioning look.

"Quick, Marta, hurry upstairs. We must wake Mrs. Kerr and Hannah. I am coming up in a moment."

The woman obeyed and Felicity turned to Evan. "Can you keep the officers down here? It is best they hear it from Henry." She took Henry's arm and they hurried up the stairs. Evan stood next to the closed door, wondering how the women would move forward.

AT SEEING HER, both Hannah and her mother immediately knew

it was bad news. Henry, bless him, did his best to tell them what he'd witnessed, the entire time wincing each time Hannah or her mother wailed.

"The police are downstairs," Felicity offered. "Would you like for me to speak to them?"

"No." Mrs. Kerr wiped at her face. "I will go down. Let me find a more presentable dressing gown."

Felicity sat on the bed next to Hannah, holding her hand as her friend cried, her entire body shaking as grief overcame her. Henry sat ramrod straight, his arm around Hannah who was inconsolable.

"I cannot believe it. I refuse to." Hannah finally managed mopping her tears with Henry's kerchief. "This cannot be true."

It took a while to coax Hannah to dress. Along with Evan and Henry, they accompanied her and her mother to the morgue.

After that, Henry left. He looked exhausted and no doubt wished to sleep and process what he'd witnessed on his own.

"We should go to my parents'. Mother will know what we should do," Felicity whispered to Evan. "I do not think it is the time to leave them alone."

It was a long day, mostly of sitting about going over scenarios of what could have happened. She and her mother oversaw the preparation of dinner and then had the servants prepare a room for Hannah and her mother after deciding they were in no state to be left alone.

Mrs. Kerr had stopped speaking, instead praying without stopping until the police arrived again. This time, they wished to ask more intrusive questions for which it was only Felicity's parents that sat with her as she spoke to them.

"Do they not wish to speak to me?" Hannah asked. "What can they wish to ask that I cannot be privy to?"

Felicity wondered if perhaps there was more of a reason than robbery for the murder. Perhaps there was more to Mr. Kerr than they'd been aware of.

"I'm sure it's just perfunctory, since she is his wife."

After the police left, Mrs. Kerr was paler and sat at a chair wiping her eyes. Felicity's father handed her a glass of brandy.

"Drink, Margaret, it will make you feel better."

She did without argument.

"I suppose once this is all sorted, we can discuss making arrangements." Her mother, always ready and first to volunteer to organize every function, said. Felicity's heart squeezed at the forlorn look of loss in both her best friend's and her mother's gazes.

"Hannah, do you wish to go to bed and rest?" Felicity waited, and when Hannah nodded, they went upstairs.

Felicity went downstairs at her and Evan's house and into the sitting room. She was greeted by Henry, Miles, and Evan all sitting in silence. Each with a brandy snifter in hand, they all seemed lost in thought. The occurrence of the day obviously was beyond words.

Felicity left them to their own devices and walked around the house to see what progress had been made. The dining room was almost complete. She peered up at the ceiling, noting it had been completely replastered. The only thing left was finishing the wallpapering and drapes.

"What are you doing?" Evan asked, coming up behind her and hugging her close. "You should prepare for bed."

Felicity turned in his arms, finally allowing herself to cry. "I cannot bear my dear friend hurting so. Why would anyone kill her father?"

"I do not know. But I do know that you must remain strong for Hannah. She will need you."

Nodding, she wiped at her eyes. "How is Henry?"

"He is here because he needs to talk about it, to go over how this came to be." Evan guided her to the doorway. "I will walk with you upstairs and instruct Ana to see about you. Rest. I will be up later." Upon entering their bedroom, he gave her a hug and kissed her gently. "Rest, darling."

Felicity could not fathom going through tough times like this without Evan's strength. She was so very fortunate.

While she slept, Evan climbed into bed and pulled her close. Death did that, she supposed, snuggling into her husband.

It brought the living closer.

EPILOGUE

T HE FACT THE morning was brighter than the days before annoyed Hannah. Her swollen eyes could barely stand daylight, but less the day being so sunny.

Somehow, she'd managed to make it through her father's funeral services without dissolving into a puddle of tears and grief.

Throughout the entire process, her dear friend Felicity had never left her side.

It was strange that the terrible murder of her father had somehow brought her and the devilishly handsome Henry to spend time together, each trying to figure out what to do next.

After the funeral, people came and went to pay respects. A ridiculous thing, she considered, to have to entertain at a time like this.

Thankfully, Felicity's mother was magical when it came to putting things together and had taken care of all that was needed.

In all probability, Felicity's parents were paying for everything, as her family had little means, especially now that the tea shop, where her father had been killed, was closed.

The din of the quiet conversations of all the people made her ears ring. How she wished everyone would go away and leave her to grieve.

"Come, let us get a breath of fresh air," Felicity said, taking her hand.

Once outside, Hannah winced at the brightness of the sun. The warmth on her skin, however, was welcome. The house felt unreasonably cold as of late. Hannah was at a loss as to what to say to Felicity. Thankfully, her friend understood, and they sat in silence on a bench.

Moments later, she noted that her mother walked among the foliage, seeming almost content. It struck Hannah as strange that she been outside most of the time and not inside with all those who came to give condolences.

"Mother, we should return inside." Hannah took her mother's arm only to be shocked when she pulled back.

"I cannot. I do not wish to. I must inform you that I am leaving. I must. This is a sign from God. He wishes me to fulfill my destiny."

"What?" Hannah looked to Felicity, who seemed just as confused. "What are you saying, Mother?"

Her mother gave her a strangely vacant smile. "I do love you, Hannah, but I do not belong here, never have. I am a woman of God. I must go to him."

"What about me?" Hannah asked. "You cannot possibly leave me alone."

Her mother waved her hand as if it was something irrelevant. "You will have the income from my inheritance. There is a bit left in savings, and your father had a small life insurance. It will do until you marry."

The urge to take her mother by the shoulders and shake her was overwhelming. "A young woman cannot live alone," she said slowly. "It is not acceptable."

Margaret Kerr's gaze hardened. "Of course, however is it more acceptable that a man and woman be forced to marry against their will? That I be torn from my true path and your father from the woman he loved? Tell me, is it?"

The wind blew across, fanning their faces with its gentle touch. It would not do to argue with her mother. In a way, the decision did not surprise her. What did was her mother's selfishness. She could not wait even a few days to tell Hannah this?

The next day, Hannah woke to find a note on a side table.

I am so happy and wish you to be as well. Be with care, daughter, follow your heart. I will pray for you always.

Mother

Next to her mother's perfectly signed name was a box. She didn't have to look inside to know what it held. It was the jewelry her father had given her mother over the years. Each time, she'd admire it and only wear it once. Then she'd claim that it would be for Hannah and she'd place it in the rather ordinary-looking wooden box.

Life alone was to begin, it seemed.

Later that morning, she sat at a desk looking over paperwork, her eyesight blurring when tears threatened.

There was a knock at the front door, and she wondered if it would be the constable returning to ask more questions, or perhaps, her mother had changed her mind.

Waving her one maid away, Hannah let out a sigh and pulled the door open.

Her life was so different now, and she couldn't help but wonder if the man who stood before her would somehow play a part.

"Please come in," she told him.

Henry Campbell stepped into the foyer. "I cannot stay long. I only came to let you know that the reason for your father's murder has come to light."

"Why was he killed?" Hannah asked.

"It is possible he owed a great deal of money and failed to pay it. If that is so, whoever the debt collector is may come after you and your mother for the balance due. You could lose everything."

Unable to keep from it, Hannah chuckled without mirth. "Of course."

Will Hannah find love amidst her mother's betrayal, a man bent on repayment, and a surprising suitor? Read A Rogue to Cherish and you will be enthralled while finding out.

ABOUT THE AUTHOR

Most days USA Today Bestseller Hildie McQueen can be found in her overly tight leggings and green hoodie, holding a cup of British black tea while stalking her hunky lawn guy. Author of Medieval Highlander and American Historical romance, she writes something every reader can enjoy.

Hildie's favorite past-times are reader conventions, traveling, shopping and reading.

She resides in beautiful small town Georgia with her super-hero husband Kurt and three little doggies.

Visit her website at www.hildiemcqueen.com
Facebook: HildieMcQueen
Twitter: @HildieMcQueen
Instagram: hildiemcqueenwriter